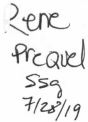

Rene
Prequel
SSg
7/28/19

MARK TAYLOR:
GENESIS

M.P. McDonald

MARK TAYLOR: GENESIS

PREQUEL IN THE MARK TAYLOR SERIES

M.P. MCDONALD

This book is a work of fiction. People, places, events, and situations are the product of the author's imagination. Any resemblance to actual persons, living or dead, or historical events, is purely coincidental

ISBN-13: 978-1492275510
ISBN-10: 1492275514

For Mom and Dad.

CHAPTER ONE ~1999

Mark Taylor paused just inside the door of the pub while his eyes adjusted to the dim interior. As excited as Mohommad had been when he had insisted on meeting here, Mark was surprised he hadn't been standing inside the door waiting for him like a little kid watching for Santa Claus. He glanced at his watch. *Damn*. He was over thirty minutes late thanks to the final shoot of the day running over, but being a fellow photographer, Mo would understand...probably.

"Mark!" Mo waved from the end of the bar and pointed to the empty stool beside him. Winding his way through the room, Mark nodded to a few acquaintances and stopped for a quick hello with a couple of others.

"Hey, Mo! How's it going?" Mark clapped him on the shoulder as he slid onto the stool. After ordering a beer, he grinned at his friend and made a rolling motion with his hand. "So...? What's up?"

"I have a deal for you." Mohommad paused while the bartender gave Mark his bottle of beer.

"Uh-oh. I'm not sure I like the sound of this. The last time you had a deal for me, it didn't turn out so well. " The beer was cold and soothed a throat hoarse from trying to keep a bunch of little kids upbeat and happy during a shoot for a stain remover ad. Over and over the kids had to slide into home plate. He hadn't had time to shower.

Dust coated his arms, and it tasted like he had breathed in half the dirt from the diamond.

Mo's thick eyebrows knit in confusion. "What time?"

"The time you begged me to take over the bridal party fitting and in return, you would do the portrait of the couple celebrating their golden anniversary? The boring fitting turned into a drunken bachelorette party."

A glint of humor lit Mohommad's eyes. "And they thought you were really a male stripper?"

Mark lifted his beer in salute. "Yep. The sweet old couple would have been a much safer gig."

"Safer?"

"Yeah, *safer*. Those ladies goosed me so many times, I had bruises for a week." Mark chuckled at the memory. The job had mostly been fun, but he enjoyed giving Mo a hard time about it when the opportunity arose. Mo owed him one on that gig. Drunken bridesmaids did not make for good group photos. He wondered if those photos had ever made it to the wedding album. He shook his head, the smile lingering. "Okay, so it wasn't exactly dangerous, but it does make me just a little leery of any of your so-called deals."

"You have to admit, the thought of you being a stripper is pretty hilarious." Mo chuckled and sipped from a glass of some kind of clear drink. Carbonation bubbles dotted the sides, so Mark ruled out water as the contents. Club soda? His friend's mood sobered. "But I swear, this deal isn't at all like that.

"Yeah? What's it going to cost me?"

Mohommad gave him a sly smile. "Not that much."

Mark raised an eyebrow and paused with the bottle tilted towards his mouth before taking a sip.

"Don't give me that look. You'll love my idea. You're always going on and on about how you want to do something special, like the photographers who get photos in *Life* magazine. I'm telling you, this is your chance. You'll be thanking me when you get a Pulitzer."

Snorting, Mark had to put the back of his hand to his nose to keep from spraying beer all over the top of the bar. He took a deep breath and laughed. *"Really?* Well, give it to me. Tell me all about this Pulitzer opportunity."

Mo took a sip of his own drink. "I'm going back to Afghanistan, and I want you to come with me."

"What?" It took a moment for Mark to process what Mo had said. "Why are you going, and more importantly, why do you want *me* to go?"

Turning sideways, Mo faced Mark. "You know how I told you my father brought us here as children so that we could have a greater opportunity, right?"

Mark nodded.

"Well, mostly it was because of my mother and sister. My mother wanted more opportunities for my sister. I don't know how, but she convinced my father and here we are." He spread his hands then clasped them loosely, regarding them for a moment as he seemed to gather his thoughts. "All my life, my mother told me how women are treated poorly in Afghanistan and how it's become even worse now. What I want to do is go and tell the women's stories through photographs."

The idea intrigued Mark, but he had at least a dozen questions. "It sounds...interesting and certainly a wonderful cause, but I need to know a little more. Like why me? Why don't you just do the photos yourself?"

Mo nodded. "I knew you'd ask that. I have a couple of reasons. The first is, it's going to be a big project. I figured two of us could cover more ground than I could alone, but the second reason is that you take amazing photographs. I take good ones, and technically, I'm probably better than you, but you have a knack for getting photos that show the soul of a person."

Mark studied his beer bottle as heat climbed his neck and raced up his face. Did Mo really think that? Elbow propped, he grasped the top of the bottle with his thumb and first two fingers, twisting it back and forth. He glanced at Mo. "When did you get so damn poetic?"

Mo's teeth flashed as he smirked. "Poetry sings through my blood, Mark. I'm so full of poetry, it almost chokes me unless I let it spill out from time to time. "

"Well, you're full of something all right, but most people wouldn't call it poetry," Mark said, but he smiled as he drained the bottle.

* * *

Mark took a deep breath as he turned his Jeep onto the long gravel driveway up to his parents' house. Flowers bloomed all around the sunny yellow house, and baskets of flowers hung at intervals along the wraparound porch. The sight was calming. Maybe his dad would keep his mouth shut about Mark's career choice. They said there was a first time for everything. He grabbed his duffle bag out of the back and exited the car, taking the steps up the front porch two at a time, the habit ingrained from childhood.

With a light knock, he opened the front door. "Mom? I'm here." He closed his eyes and sniffed. Apple pie? He grinned.

"In the kitchen, hon!"

Dropping the duffle at the bottom of the step, he ambled down the hallway to the kitchen. "Hey, Mom." He threw an arm over her shoulder and snatched a bit of crust off the edge of the pie cooling on the counter.

"Hey, hands off! That's for dessert." She gave his hand a light smack, but he just laughed, already scheming how he could get a slice before dinner.

"Do you have ice cream?"

"No, sorry."

A pang of disappointment was short-lived as his mother gave him a sly smile. There was ice cream, he was sure of it.

"Where's Dad?"

His mom waved vaguely towards the backyard. "He's out there sharpening…something. I forget what."

"Is he on-call tonight?" Part of him was hoping his father would have to leave, but guilt stabbed him even as the thought dashed through his mind. He couldn't avoid telling his parents about his upcoming trip so he steeled his resolve to break the news tonight no matter what.

His mother opened the fridge and pulled out a tray of hamburgers and another of fresh vegetables. "The grill is about ready. Would you go throw these on?"

Mark took the trays. "Sure." He wasn't much of a chef, but he could handle burgers on the grill. The zucchini and summer squash were a little more challenging. After tossing the burgers on, and setting the sliced veggies around the edges of the grill, he leaned against the deck railing. The backyard met a cornfield at the far end. Towards late summer, the stalks would tower over his head and playing hide and seek had been an irresistible temptation for him and his friends—until they incurred the wrath of the farmer who lived on the other side of the field. His father had hung up the phone after speaking with the farmer and given Mark the 'Look'. After that, they could only go into the corn to look for a lost baseball. They lost a lot of them.

"Thirsty?"

Mark turned, his mind so focused on the past, he gave a mental start when he saw the beer his mom held out in offering. "Sure. Thanks." He cracked it open and took a long swallow. The burgers sizzled so he lifted one to see if it needed flipping. Not quite.

She had a glass of iced tea and took a seat on the lounger. "So, what brings you up here this weekend?"

Mark shrugged. "Can't a guy just want to visit his parents without having a reason?"

"Of course, but you have something up your sleeve. I can tell." She sipped her tea, her eyes thoughtful. "Is it a girl?"

He cringed at the hope in her voice. If she had her wish, he would be married off and have at least four kids by now. It was no secret that she had always wanted more kids. "Sorry. There's nobody special at the moment." He dated occasionally, always searching for the right woman, but so far, none had whatever it was he was seeking. His parents told him he was too picky and maybe he was, but it was more than that. It was as if he was missing something and had to find the woman who held whatever it was he was missing—like a crazy scavenger hunt, only he had no map or clue as to where to begin the hunt. "Anyway, it's nothing major, just a trip I'm planning with Mohommad. He came out to dinner that one time."

"Sure, I remember him. Where are you going on your trip?"

The smoke from the burgers wafted in the breeze, the aroma making his mouth water. He turned them over. "I'll fill you in over dinner. Do you want me to go get Dad, or do you want to?"

She set her iced tea on a side table, stood and held her hand out for the spatula. "I'll take over."

Mark surprised his father in the woodshop, and took a few moments to admire the bookcase his dad was working on. Some guys liked to relax by working on cars, or watching sports, but his dad's hobby was woodworking. For years his father tried to get Mark interested, and while he could build a birdhouse or a simple bookcase, his heart had never been in it. He'd rather take a photo of the tree than carve it into something.

Over dinner, Mark's dad told stories about work, asked Mark if he was coming up in the fall for their annual hunting trip and finally, almost grudgingly, inquired as to how Mark's photography business was going.

"It's going great, Dad. I'm getting some good commercial jobs. I even shot a national print ad for a major diaper brand." That job had allowed him to make his last loan payment for the photography equipment he had needed when he started the business. He might not earn close to what his dad earned as a doctor, but he was self-sufficient and building a nice cushion.

"Diapers? *Really?*"

Mark bit back the burn of resentment his father's tone ignited. On the surface, a diaper ad did sound kind of silly, but it paid big bucks and was a lot more work than his dad would ever understand. Babies didn't perform on command. Granted, it wasn't the cover of *Life* or *Time* magazine, but he hoped his trip would provide him some shots that might be worth submitting.

His mother glared at his dad, then turned to Mark. "I bet chasing after those babies was quite a task."

He gave her a grateful smile. "Yeah, it was exasperating, but kind of fun too. It kept me on my toes, that's for sure, because you just never know what a baby is going to do next. If I'm not alert...bam! I miss the money shot. I mean, it's not like I can ask the baby to repeat the action." Despite the undercurrent of resentment, his enthusiasm bubbled up when describing the shoot.

To his credit, his dad laughed at some of the antics Mark recalled and by the time his mother brought the apple pie to the table, the mood had mellowed.

She handed him a carton of vanilla ice cream and the scooper. "Look what I found in the back of the freezer."

Grinning, he dug the ice cream scooper into the carton and plopped a scoop on his dad's slice of pie, and then his own. His mom passed. Mark shrugged. "You're missing out, Mom." With the edge of his fork, he sawed off a mouthful of pie, making sure to get some ice cream in the bite. The apples, lightly browned with cinnamon, were still warm, and their tart flavor was balanced by the cold ice cream. Heaven on a plate.

"That's okay. I'm not even sure I can eat this piece, I'm so full." She took a small bite and then looked at Mark with her eyebrows raised. "So, did you have something special you wanted to tell us while you were here?"

Lifting one shoulder, he edged off another bite, and said, "It really isn't that big of a deal. I'm going to Afghanistan with Mohommad. He has a great idea for a book, and he wants me to do most of the photography."

Mark jumped when his dad's fork clattered onto the table. "You're going to Afghanistan? Are you out of your *mind*?"

He had expected skepticism but not the vehemence his father displayed. "No, it's a great opportunity. It's the kind of photography I've always wanted to do."

"The country is unstable. Even the Red Cross is pulling a lot of their workers out of the country after a bunch of them were beaten. Didn't you see that on the news?"

Poking at the edge of the crust with his fork, Mark nodded. "Sure. I heard about it, but that doesn't mean something like that is going to happen to me. Mohommad has family there. His uncle is some kind of mayor or whatever they call it, of his village."

With a grunt, his dad picked up his fork and polished off his pie, his jaw working it as if the crust was leather instead of delicate, flaky pastry. "What about your business? Do you think you can really go off and just leave it?"

"I don't know why you're so dead set against this before you even hear me out." He slid his plate away and glared at his dad. "I'm kind of surprised that you're concerned about my business since you've never shown an interest in it before." Immediately he regretted his remark and sighed, scrubbing his hands against his eyes before spreading them. "Look, I just feel like it's something I have to do, okay? I may never get another chance like this and as far as my studio goes, the trip is planned for July. That's my slowest time. People are busy or out of town, and the fall print ads haven't started yet. It's the best time of year for me to go. Besides, I have a little money saved up, and Mo is paying for most of the expenses in return for me doing most of the photos. It's like a working vacation."

His mother touched his hand and said, "Mark, we're just worried that something could happen. Couldn't you go somewhere like Europe?"

"No." What was there for him to photograph in Europe? French women walking their dogs down the Champs Elysee? Italian women catering to their forty-year old sons? He took a deep breath. "Look, while I agree there might be *some* risk, it's not like I'm going into battle. Mohommad wants to do a book about the plight of women in Afghanistan. They are almost prisoners in their homes. They can't drive, the girls can't go to school, and basically the women are the property of their husbands." He saw a hint of understanding in his mother's eyes, but his dad was leaning back, his arms crossed, obviously still skeptical. He tried one more time. "Don't you understand? Mohommad intends to help the women of Afghanistan with the book. It's a chance for me to do something good. I know it doesn't compare to being a doctor, but I think I can help make a difference.

Nobody spoke and only the sound of the clock ticking on the soffit above the sink broke the silence until Mark said, "You realize that I'm not asking permission. I'm just asking for your blessing, but either way, I'm going."

His parents exchanged a look across the table. Mark wasn't sure exactly what they said in their unspoken communication, but they must have come to a conclusion because his mother nodded to his father.

"You're a grown man, so we can't stop you even if we tried, but if you feel you have to go, there isn't much we can do to change your mind. Just stay safe."

The muscles in Mark's neck eased. He hadn't been aware of how knotted they had been until they relaxed. Almost giddy with relief, Mark nodded. "I intend to.

Mohommad has been back to visit several times in the last few years, so he knows where it's safe to go and where it isn't. Plus, he already has an itinerary planned for us."

For the next hour, Mark spoke of Mohommad's plans and his father offered advice here and there, while his mom reminded him of items he would want to pack. Most of their suggestions were just common sense ones that Mark would have done anyway, but he thanked them nonetheless, and pretended that he would never have thought of those things without their help.

CHAPTER TWO

Mark slung his camera bag across his chest, one hand resting on it as he and Mohommad navigated the teeming streets of Kandahar.

Tan. That was his first impression of the city. The color dominated the landscape — from the jagged mountains in the distance to the dusty ground beneath his feet, but as he took in the streets up close, he realized that splashes of color were everywhere and the crystalline blue sky seemed endless. Motorbikes, cars and bicycles fought for dominance on the roads, and if there were traffic rules, Mark couldn't figure them out. It looked like a free-for-all.

A figure covered head-to-toe in blue cloth passed him and he tried not to stare. Mohommad had briefed him on the laws of Afghanistan, but it was one thing to hear that women had to wear the stifling burqas, but to see it close-up was unsettling. How did the women even see where they were going? It went beyond merely a veil. In the burqas, even the women's eyes were covered, and only a rectangular window covered in a mesh of sorts, kept the women from being blind under the garment.

His shirt stuck to his chest as the heat beat down from the sky and radiated up from the pavement. He pulled it away from his body and wondered how the women managed not to faint dressed as they were. As they passed a street vendor selling some kind of food, it crossed his mind that eating in public must be difficult or impossible. Maybe they only ate at home? Mohommad said they only had to wear the burqas in public.

The camera case bumped against his side and he steadied it. His travel visa allowed him to take photos only of landscapes not people, and especially not women, but Mo had assured him that once out of the city they would be able to use the cameras without worrying about Taliban watching. While members of the militant group lived in the smaller villages too, everyone knew who they were and so Mo said it would be challenging, but possible to avoid them. The fact that they had to basically sneak photos had Mark uneasy, but Mohommad didn't seem worried and had relatives who said they would help arrange photo opportunities.

Their hotel looked like it had once been opulent, but after years of war and inner strife, its best days were behind it. Far, far behind it. Mark didn't care. He was so tired from the flight which had two layovers, he just washed up and slept like the dead. The next morning, they ate a light breakfast of scrambled eggs, which weren't much different than he was used to eating, except these had tomatoes in them. They rounded out the breakfast with fruit, nuts and tea, and although he would have preferred coffee, the tea went well with the fruit.

"So, are we heading out to your uncle's home today?" Mark popped the last grape in his mouth.

Mohommad nodded as he drained his tea and set the cup down. "Yes, they live a bit north of here. We'll go there, and tonight there will be lots of food and celebrating. Tomorrow, we'll go out and begin working on photos for the book."

"Sounds good."

* * *

Mark sat on the floor with Mo's uncles and cousins and shook off with a smile another entreaty by Mo's uncle to eat more. His stomach already felt like it was going to burst, but he almost wished he had room. The food was delicious. They had dined while sitting on the floor and eating from communal bowls filled with lamb kebabs and some kind of rice with raisins, small slices of carrots and pistachios which he scooped up and ate with a toasted sesame seed flatbread. Fruit was offered at the end of the meal while tea was once again the beverage of choice. Tea had never been a favorite beverage, but it was beginning to grow on him.

He sipped it and glanced around the room. The home itself had reminded him almost of the mud homes that Pueblo people of the U.S. Southwest had lived in, except this one was surrounded by a high wall. Mo had explained that his cousins all lived within the compound with their families too. Mark couldn't keep straight who was who and he wasn't sure exactly of the living arrangements, but children were everywhere, the sound of their laughing and playing filling the house.

Women had been present and served the meal, but they had left the room and Mark assumed they ate elsewhere. Sleeping arrangements hadn't been made clear to him yet either, and he blinked with fatigue. A pile of blankets occupied one corner of the room. The only thing he knew was that everyone slept on the floor, which was fine with him.

The men around him all burst into laughter and he wished he could follow the conversation. If he could, he knew he wouldn't feel so sleepy, but while everyone was welcoming and friendly, he felt out of place. Although several of the men spoke English, they all were speaking Pashto now, even Mo. While Mark had known that English was not Mo's native tongue, it was still strange listening to his friend converse in his own language. It was as if he became someone else. His mannerisms changed along with the tone and inflection in his voice. In his first language, he was no longer Mo, but Mohommad.

* * *

The next morning, after a surprisingly restful night on a thin mattress on the floor, Mark and Mohommad loaded their cameras into the back of their vehicle. The plan was to visit some neighboring villages where Mohommad had some distant relatives. Two of Mo's cousins, Faisal and Sayeed, were going to accompany them. The men were a bit younger than Mo, and had seemed friendly enough the evening before.

While Mark checked to make sure all his lenses had come through the trip unscathed, Mo stepped close and said, "My cousins speak English very well, and they think we are only here to take photos of how life is in Afghanistan. I've insisted that we need pictures of everyone, including the women so that we can show the people in America the truth about the beauty of this country, but they weren't too thrilled about having to ask the men in the village for permission to photograph the women. It might help that I remember some of the men, but you're a foreigner and not Muslim. You might have to sit tight until we know for sure if it's okay."

Mark zipped his bag shut and glanced over his shoulder to make sure the cousins weren't within hearing distance and was satisfied that they were filling water bottles at the well.

"Why did you bring me if I can't photograph women? I mean, you're from here, right?" He couldn't help the spark of anger. While the trip itself was amazing, his real excitement had been the thrill of participating in an effort to make a difference in the women's lives. He hadn't expected to effect any real change, but buried beneath all the doubt and rationality had been a scrap of hope that maybe, just maybe, the book would help in some small way.

Mohommad pulled back, his eyes narrowing. "Yes, I was born here, but I was just a child when I left. I've only been back a few times since then. You saw the bullet holes and the ruined buildings in Kandahar. It isn't high on anyone's list of vacation destinations, including *my* family's. Given the choice, my father took us to Disney World."

Mark broke eye contact and rubbed the back of his neck. "Look...I'm sorry. That was stupid of me."

Shrugging, Mohommad waved off the apology. "No problem. You'll get your chance. Besides, I also need photos of the homes and conditions here, not just the women. Those photos will help set the tone of the book and give it context."

Mark nodded, but he wasn't completely satisfied. Mo took fantastic landscapes and certainly didn't need any help in that regard.

The drive was bone-jarring and Faisal drove like a colony of bats were chasing them out of the depths of hell. Mark swiped his arm across his forehead. Maybe the hell association stemmed from the heat. He was used to hot, humid Chicago summers, but this was like a blast furnace. His teeth felt like they were going to rattle right out of his head. The ride would take about forty-five minutes, which had surprised him when Mo relayed the news. This was the definition of a neighboring village?

With all the bumps and jolts, Mark soon gave up all attempts at conversation and instead settled back to observe the scenery. The raw beauty of the landscape made him forget the heat. The air had a quality he couldn't define—it was as though he had been looking through a dusty window his whole life and suddenly, it had been wiped clean. Everything was so crisp, despite the dust. Distance was deceptive and Mark was sure he could have thrown a baseball and it would reach the mountains, but he chuckled at the idea even as it crossed his mind. The mountains were miles away. Growing up in Wisconsin, he wasn't used to mountains, only rolling hills, but he had traveled a bit and gone skiing in Colorado a few times. His dad had also taken the family on vacation to the Grand Canyon one year. Maybe Afghanistan looked so different because there was less pollution.

He sipped from his canteen of water. Despite the insulated cover, the water was already warm, but dust coated the inside of his mouth so he took another sip. He'd have to get used to it for the next few weeks because in the dry heat, it would be easy to get dehydrated. At least his Cubs baseball hat would provide him some protection from the sun. He had a month or so to acquire a tan in Chicago before the trip, but he had a feeling it might not make much difference and was glad for the loose long-sleeved cotton shirt Mo had recommended instead of the simple t-shirt Mark had been planning to wear.

At the first village, he stepped from the vehicle and stretched, working some kinks out of his neck as he swept his tongue over his teeth, half-expecting to discover a few loose fillings. Finding everything still secure, he forgot his minor discomfort from the drive as he took in his surroundings. The mouth-watering scent of roasting meat vied for dominance over the pungent scent of sheep and the vague smell of something rotten. High-walled compounds surrounded the center of the village with a spot of green nearby where Mo had explained the village shared a large common vegetable garden. It surprised him to find it in the middle of the village, but he guessed it needed to be near the water source. From doing some of his own studying, he knew that the compounds usually housed three or four related families.

The men of the village were eager to show them around, proudly showing their herds of sheep. It seemed the women were always just out of sight. A few ventured out in their burqas, but the only other glimpse he had was a flash of movement in a few doorways when he would turn. He had the feeling of being watched, but it wasn't an ominous feeling of being spied upon, it was more one of curiosity. He just wished one woman would pause for a second so he could snap her picture. Faisal tugged on Mark's arm and pointed to some children playing near the well. They kicked a clod of dirt back and forth as though it was a soccer ball and it soon become apparent that the goal of the game was to destroy the clod, but only through kicking it. When one boy inadvertently stepped on it, the others shouted and shoving ensued. Faisal laughed and said something to the other men. Smiles and chuckles lit their faces even though the guilty clod smasher was beneath the pile of other boys. Mark took a step towards them. He didn't have a plan, but the unfairness of the other boys piling on compelled him to try to break up the fight, but Mo blocked him with an outstretched arm.

"Don't interfere. This is how it is with children. They learn to defend themselves at an early age here."

"But it's five against one," Mark said, keeping his voice as even as he could, not wanting to cause a scene. "What if he gets hurt?"

Mo laughed. "Then he'll learn to either fight harder next time, or become more nimble on his feet so that he doesn't ruin the game."

At that moment, the boy emerged from beneath the pile, having somehow wiggled out. Instead of running, he laughed, wiped a trickle of blood from his nose, and shouted something to the others. Mark couldn't understand the words, but he needed no translation for the tone. The boy was clearly saying the Pashto equivalent of 'Suckers!'

Embarrassed, Mark shrugged. "I guess you were right."

Mo nodded as his face split into a grin. "You know I always am."

"Shut up." Mark smiled and lifted his camera, snapping a succession of shots of the boys as they kicked a new clod to begin a new game.

Out of the corner of his eye, he caught a flash of movement and pivoted, surprised to see a woman peering at him from an open gate to one of the compounds. Years of photography had honed his ability to react to a good shot, and without thinking, he zoomed in and was able to squeeze off several frames of the young woman. Her eyes, wide and green, were unguarded for a split second before a veil of fear dropped down and she lowered her gaze and ducked back within the compound. It was too late. All

Mark had required was that split second. He had the first of the photos for the book. Elated, he grinned at Mo. "Did you see that?"

It wasn't Mo who answered, but rather Faisal as he gave Mark a shove. "What are you doing taking photographs of a woman?"

Stumbling sideways, Mark caught his balance and suppressed the impulse to shove the guy right back. It only took a second for his temper to cool and then he closed his eyes briefly and shook his head. Here he was, their guest, and he had already broken the rules. "I...uh...I was taking a photo of the house and I didn't see her until afterward. I apologize."

Faisal glared and Sayeed stood a step behind him, arms crossed.

Mo moved close, shooting Mark a dark look before he turned to his cousins, a smile replacing the scowl as he put a hand on Faisal's chest. "It was an accident. I won't use that photo. It's just that Mark sometimes gets too focused on his work and doesn't pay attention like he should." Then he grinned. "Focused. Get it?" He gave his cousin's shoulder a light slap. "Come on. I want to see the new well."

Mark capped his camera in frustration. Sweat trickled down his back as he trudged after the small group and tried to work up the enthusiasm to marvel at the well. He appreciated the significance of it, especially for the women, as it made their lives easier, but he just wished he wasn't hogtied in regards to his photography. As the day wore on and women scurried into their respective compounds when Mo's group approached, his frustration mounted. Faisal and Sayeed never mentioned them, and Mo ignored them too.

How was he going to photograph ghosts? Because that is what the women seemed to be to him. Blue colored ghosts. Even their feet were almost impossible to see beneath the yards of cloth and it gave the impression that they floated over the ground.

As the day progressed, it was more of the same. The only women he saw served them food in bowls and retreated to another area to eat. At least, he assumed they ate. He took countless photos of the homes, sheep, gardens, a few young boys roughhousing, and the men of the village, but he never had an opportunity to take another photo of a woman in that village.

* * *

Mark lay on the pad and scratched his chin, cursing the beard Mo had suggested he grow to fit in better. It made sense to grow it, but that didn't mean he had to like it. In the ten days they had been in the country, he had acquired a deep tan and with his dark hair and green eyes, he could be mistaken for an Afghani. At least until he spoke, but he learned to keep his mouth shut and observe. He had picked up a few words and Mo translated when he could, so he wasn't totally lost in the conversations, but after a while, he found that the other men forgot about him. This worked to his advantage and allowed him to occasionally catch a glimpse of the women.

With a last satisfying scratch, he turned onto his side and yawned. He pushed aside the worry that they wouldn't obtain enough photos for the book. It had plagued him to the point he feared that his obsession with spotting the women would be noticed and misinterpreted, but Mo didn't seem to have the same problem with the lack of opportunity. In fact, he had hardly taken any photos of anything the whole trip and when Mark had asked him about it, Mo had shrugged and said all in good time.

Other than Mo, the only people Mark could speak to directly were Faisal and Sayeed but neither man was the talkative type, moreover, they didn't seem to like him, and he had no idea why. More than once, when he approached while the two had been deep in conversation with Mo, they had stopped speaking or switched to Pashto. If they were talking about him and had a complaint, he wished Mo would clue him in, but whenever he asked, his friend laughed and said the conversations had nothing to do with him. Mark wasn't so sure, but he had to take Mo's word for it. Besides, he couldn't think of anything he had done that would cause the men to take offense except for the one incident when he had taken the woman's photograph and the cousins had caught him. He just wished he had a little more freedom to explore. The villages had compounds and the women stayed within the walls most of the time except to come out and get water from the central well a few times a day. Even if he felt comfortable shooting those images, there was nothing inherently tragic about a woman drawing water from a well.

* * *

Mark exited the car, glad to stretch his legs after a few hours in the cramped vehicle that probably hadn't ever had new shocks. They had stopped in front of mud fort on a hill overlooking a city. Squinting at the map, he picked out their location, Kunduz. Their travels had taken them to the northeast corner of the country. He folded the map and stuck it in his camera bag. Other than Kandahar, it was the biggest town he had seen. Beyond the rows of squat tan buildings interspersed with straw huts and even tents, he made out hazy hills. Kabul was to their southwest and would be the next stop, before they completed the roughly triangular travels. They would spend their last few days in Afghanistan in Kandahar to give them a two day cushion to make their flight.

Mo had another uncle who was some kind of leader in Kunduz, but Mark wasn't quite sure what post he held. He turned as Mo shut the door and moved up beside him.

As they were apparently within walking distance of their destination, Faisal and Sayeed drove off in the other direction with plans to meet them later. Mark breathed a sigh of relief. It was rare to be out of their sight, and Mark had felt a constant tension whenever they were around. He hoped they took their time doing whatever it was they were going to do.

"It's not quite Chicago, is it?"

Mark smiled. "I didn't come here to see Chicago." He swept his arm out. "This whole place is incredibly different from what I'm used to and that's what I'd hoped—what I expected. If it was just like Chicago, I could have stayed home."

"True. While it is not Chicago, someday, I pray it will be great again. Did you know Marco Polo traveled through Afghanistan on his route to China?"

"No. What little I know of Marco Polo comes from a Gary Jennings novel." He laughed.

As he and Mo descended the hill, kicking up plumes of dust with every step, he tried not to be disappointed with the ugliness of the town.

The main road was paved, but the side street they took was just dirt and they had to skirt several broken down vehicles abandoned on the road. If Jennings had described Kunduz anywhere in his book, it must have been described much differently. Of course, he would have tried to depict the town as it might have been five hundred years ago. As they passed a square mud brick house, he somehow had the feeling it probably hadn't changed all that much.

The heat pressed down on them, and Mark guessed the temperature had to be close to a hundred. He thought by now he would be used to it, but he wasn't. Sure, Chicago had its share of hot days in the summer and the humidity could make it stifling, but there was always an air conditioned restaurant, home or even a store close at hand where someone walking could go to get out of the heat. Here, it was just hot all the time. Mo told him the winters were cold, but that was hard to believe.

Thankfully, their visit to the town would be short, only a day, but that made Mark wonder why they had bothered. They stayed with Mo's uncle on his father's side, and he supposed that was why they had come this way instead of going directly to Kabul.

If Mo's uncle had a wife, Mark never saw her in the day they spent in Kunduz. They ate a meager meal and Mark felt guilty for eating any of it and possibly taking food out of the mouths of the few children he spotted. Mo's uncle spoke English and asked Mark about Chicago while they ate.

"Mohommad tells me that Chicago is beautiful. Someday, maybe I will go there."

Mark finished chewing and nodded. "It is beautiful. The lake and the skyline are amazing."

24

"Do you live in a skyscraper? Sears Tower, maybe?"

Grinning, Mark shook his head. "No. I have just an apartment above my studio. I like it though. It's an older building converted to lofts."

The uncle's eyebrows knit in confusion and Mark realized he had used terms probably unfamiliar to someone in Afghanistan. "It's nice. A few miles from the Sears Tower, but I've been up in it before. The view from the observation deck is incredible."

"Maybe someday you can send me a picture of it, no? My nephew says you are a great photographer."

Mark shrugged. "Your nephew exaggerates, but sure, I could send you a photo."

After the meal, Mo excused himself to go visit with some of his uncle's friends. "I hope you don't mind, Mark. I know you came all the way here and I feel like I am abandoning you. I can stay if you want."

"No, it's fine. I'm exhausted. I think I might hit the sack early." He had no desire to explore Kunduz.

The next morning, they left for Kabul. In the car, Mo seemed preoccupied and spoke only a little on the long drive. Mark tried to start a few conversations only to receive one word answers. Finally, he turned away and stared out the window as the mountains slid away in the distance beyond the dry steppes and wondered if he had done something to offend his friend. Had he said something inappropriate to Mo's uncle?

In Kabul, Mo seemed to come out of his funk. While they walked, Mark became aware that he finally had a chance to take photos without the watchful eyes of the cousins, who had remained in Kunduz. He pulled his camera out of the case and unzipped the top of the bag that held his three hundred millimeter lens so it would be handy if he found he needed it.

Blue burqas accompanied by men that Mark knew must be a male relative, dotted the long stretch of road, but all seemed to be on missions from one place to another.

Mark jumped when a truck roared down the street, the bed full of men carrying guns. "What the hell?"

The truck swerved to the side of the road near a lone woman. Mark was sure a man had been with the woman a few seconds ago, but now he was nowhere to be seen.

Mo pulled Mark into an alley. "Better not to catch their attention."

Mark nodded, but peered around the corner, feeling in the bag for the lens. He screwed it on and began snapping photos as two of the men shouted at the woman. She cowered, but didn't attempt to flee. Hampered by the burqa; she had no chance against them.

He flinched in shock when one of the men lifted a club and brought it down across the woman's back. The thud of wood against flesh wasn't loud, but in his mind, the sound was amplified until it resonated like a gunshot. He lowered the camera and took two steps around the corner. He had no plan of action in mind but he couldn't just stand here and watch a woman being beaten by two men.

Mo grabbed his arm. "What are you doing?"

Yanking his arm out of Mo's grasp, Mark glared at him. "What does it look like? We have to go help her."

Moving close, Mo put an arm out, blocking Mark's way. "No, we don't. Think of yourself as a reporter—you can't be part of the news, you just have to record it."

Frustration, anger and helplessness battled inside of him. Part of him realized Mo was right. They were here to record this exact kind of treatment. Knowing Mo was correct was one thing—accepting it was a different matter. Even as he watched, people on the street walked past the commotion. Men would stop to look for a few seconds, but the women would pass without faltering. Were they so used to these scenes that they were no longer affected? Mark didn't see how that was possible and guessed they were terrified of being the next victim, and that ignoring it was their best defense.

"You can't help, Mark. You are a foreigner and your 'help' could end up getting her killed and you arrested."

For a split second, he didn't care about getting arrested. It was gut response, but common sense finally slapped him upside the head. If he were arrested, it would defeat their purpose. Resolutely, Mark nodded, but the muscles in his jaw tightened as he lifted the camera and caught the end of the conflict.

The woman tumbled to the ground.

Click.

Another blow with the club.

Click.

The men shouted at her, prodding her with their feet.

Click.

Shakily, she stumbled to her feet, and made her way to the truck, where she was loaded in the back. She huddled in a shapeless blue heap in a corner of the bed as the men jumped on the running boards. The vehicle sped away. *Click. Click. Click.*

Mark lowered the camera, shaking with anger as he stared after the truck. He recapped his lens and dropped it back in the case, jerking the zipper closed. Ignoring his natural instinct to intervene had been like trying to ignore the instinct to breathe. An empty bottle caught his eye and with a muttered curse, he kicked it into the side of the building. The explosion of glass against the bricks didn't satisfy his anger, but the shards scattered on the ground added to his guilt. He had seen dozens of kids running around the town, rooting around in the garbage and now one might cut their foot because of him. He bent, sliding his arm into the camera strap so that it draped diagonally across his chest, and picked up the pieces.

"Leave it, Mark. It's not going to matter."

He would have argued, but a glance around him showed no trash receptacles anywhere around and Mo was right. It wouldn't matter. His wasn't the only glass around. He dropped the shards, disgusted with himself, the men who had beaten the woman, and the country in general.

He tried to reason in his mind that at least he had captured the beating on film. When people saw the photographs, maybe he would help shed some light on the atrocities committed. Change seemed like it was an unreachable goal and impossible for him to achieve. Tradition and culture was ingrained over hundreds, if not thousands of years, and he was just a guy who took pictures. It wasn't like he had any real power to make things better.

He straightened, brushing his hands together and slanted a glance at Mo. "So now what's going to happen to her?" he asked, inclining his head in the direction of where the beating had taken place.

Mo regarded him for a long moment and then his eyes slid away. "I'm not sure."

His friend's evasive action hinted at the truth. "Bullshit."

* * *

Kabul was large and busy, but showed signs of the war that had torn the country apart. It wasn't as scarred as Kandahar, but it was not untouched. Mo showed little interest in taking photos, so Mark stole away whenever he could and wondered where the material for a book would come from. His friend didn't seem to be taking notes either.

The lack of effort drove Mark to seek even more snapshots as he felt the more he took of this way of life, the better his chance of making a difference, with or without Mo. He learned to be stealthy, and pretended to photograph other objects, but shifted the focus at the last moment. None of the photographs were as brutal as the beating, but as the town was larger than the villages they had passed through so he was able to get more glimpses of women venturing to the market. What frustrated him was his inability to capture on film the sense that the women were basically invisible in their burqas.

A few men glared at him, and once when he tried to take a photo of a woman, an apparent beggar with two small children, the mother covered the children's' faces with her own burqa. He tried to apologize to her, but she gathered her children and left the area. He cursed his stupidity as she hurried away. Of course she couldn't acknowledge his apology. Not only had she probably not understood it, she wasn't allowed to speak to strange men.

The inequality struck him like a clenched fist and once he knew it was there, it was all he could see. Vendors would ignore a woman and take care of a male customer even if the woman was there first. Other little things stuck with him, like how the schools in the town were full of little boys. Groups of boys from very young to teenagers would trek alongside the roads, to the madrassa, but little girls were absent. He had known these things before arriving in Afghanistan, but it had been an abstract knowledge. Seeing it firsthand made it real, but also incomprehensible.

Faisal and Sayeed seemed to have other duties in their hometown. In the evenings, they left the home. Mo said they were visiting other relatives. Mark didn't really care, he was just glad they were gone.

On the night before they left Kabul, Mo informed him that he had to go to a village far from town with the cousins. It was a family thing. Mo suggested that Mark ride back to Kandahar with a friend of the family and wait for Mo there. Mark got the hint. He wasn't welcome, but he didn't care. He finally felt he had some decent photos and their flight home couldn't come quickly enough. He had experienced his fill of violence, heat, and dust. Chicago traffic and humidity would seem insignificant after this trip.

The almost twenty-four hour long trip back to Kandahar had been uncomfortable. Physically, the nearly five hundred miles had seemed endless. There were no roadside oasis stops like in the United States. No McDonalds' or Burger Kings and not even any truck stops. The roads took them through desert and mountains. They brought their own food and water and made only a few stops to refuel and take a quick leak.

When he arrived back in Kandahar, the relative arranged for Mark to stay at the hotel he and Mo had stayed at the first night. That was no small feat, as most of the hotels had been destroyed in the years of war, so Mark tried to convey his appreciation. As much as he hated the treatment of the women here, he couldn't fault the hospitality he had received. These people didn't even know him, and yet he had been fed and driven around the country. Mark wanted to pay the man, but he insisted Mo had taken care of everything already, so Mark smiled and thanked the man one more time before he headed into his room and flopped on the bed with a weary sigh. Just a few more days, and then he'd be home.

He slept late the next day, glad that he had nothing on his agenda. It was his plan to get an early start to the day and take more photographs, but the last few weeks finally caught up with him and it was almost eleven when he woke up. After washing and dressing, he took his camera, making sure his batteries were still good and he had plenty of film. Today he planned to just be a sightseer—a tourist of sorts, although the country probably hadn't seen many tourists in the last twenty years or so. While he had visited many places, he hadn't had a chance to really go out and explore on his own and he relished the opportunity.

By now, his beard was full, and he had acquired probably the darkest tan of his life, allowing him to blend with the populace as long as he didn't have to speak to anyone. As he wandered about Kabul, his camera at his side, he noticed the women beggars along the side of the road. Mo had mentioned that the women who had no husband or male relatives had a hard life, but he hadn't expected that so many had to rely on begging. He took a few photos of them, and then dropped some coins in their cups.

Growing up, the women's lib movement had been a big political hot button topic, but Mark had been just a kid and it was irrelevant to his life. He played baseball, rode bikes and teased girls in his neighborhood by chasing them with worms or nasty bugs he found in the corn. When he was old enough to ditch the worms and just chase them figuratively, equal rights for women meant he didn't have to open doors for them—except his parents had drilled the courtesy into him practically from the crib—so he was left confused as to what he was supposed to do. Hold doors? Pay for dates? He usually went with his instincts, which meant following his father's example.

Even when he went to college, women's lib for him was more about liberating a girl from her clothes than in any political movement.

Mark discovered even if Mo didn't follow up finishing the book, he knew this trip would change the way he thought of women for the rest of his life. At least it wouldn't be a waste in that regard. Instead of erasing his frustration, the prospect of not being able to show the world what was going on set off a slow, simmering anger.

* * *

Mid-afternoon the city slowed down as people retreated from the heat and Mark did the same, sitting in the shade of a building as he bit into a plum he had bought from a vendor. The juice squirted in his mouth, and he had to admit that the fruit in this country tasted better than any he could remember. It could have been because he hadn't eaten any junk food for several weeks and his tastes were changing, or maybe because the fruit assuaged his thirst as well. He wiped his mouth with the back of his hand, stopping when a small boy approached him. The boy's clothes hung in tatters and his feet were bare. The child sank onto his haunches and smiled at him, showing a gap-toothed grin. Mark returned the smile, pegging his age at about seven given the lack of teeth. Taking a last bite of the plum, Mark set it beside him, noticing the boy's eyes glued to the pit. He reached into his pocket and produced the other two plums and bag of almonds he had purchased.

He offered them to the boy. "Are you hungry?"

The boy's dark eyes shot to Mark's at the words and Mark knew he'd given away his foreigner status. Would that scare the boy away? Apparently it didn't, because it didn't take much prodding before the boy accepted the gifts. He sat beside Mark and dug into the food, which surprised Mark until he noticed the boy's anxious glances down the street. A group of ragged boys were coming their way. The group shouted something at the boy, who shouted back and took another huge bite of the plum, making Mark worry that he'd choke on the fruit.

Although he couldn't understand what the boys were saying to each other, he understood the tone and body language. The biggest boy in the group was demanding the food and the little one beside Mark was trying to consume as much of it as he could before having to give up his prize. Always one to root for the underdog, Mark stood and glared at the boys. He felt like a big bully as he towered over them, but on the other hand, they would certainly understand the concept, as they bullied the younger boy. They backed off, turning to head back the way they had come, but not before shouting something at the little boy. Mark hoped he hadn't made anything worse for the kid, but a glance down showed the boy had already dismissed the group from his mind while he fished in the bag of almonds.

With nothing else pressing to do, Mark decided to stick around and guard the boy until he was done eating, but when the child finished, he stood and tugged on Mark's sleeve and pointed down the opposite direction from where the other boys had gone.

"What? You want me to go that way?" Mark asked, pointing down the road.

The boy smiled and yanked on Mark's arm again, until laughing, Mark went along with him. "Fine. I've got nothing to do today. Show me your city."

Their first stop was the market and Mark bought some more fruit and nuts for the boy, along with a kabob of lamb and vegetables for each of them. They ate as they walked, with the boy keeping up a running commentary that Mark didn't understand.

Before he knew it, he was on the outskirts of the city and the ruins of a citadel stood before them. Mark uncapped his camera and took photos of it. The sun was on its downward trek in the western sky and lit the citadel with a soft light. Snapping away, Mark stopped to thank the boy but he was gone. He missed the chatter, but was glad he'd been able to at least give the kid a decent meal.

After taking a dozen photographs from several different angles, Mark decided to head back to his hotel. He didn't want to be caught outside its safety after dark. He'd learned that much while he was here. Mo had warned him that the Taliban ruled most of the country and people out after dark were at risk. It still puzzled Mark that Mo appeared to have accomplished very little in regards to the book, and his sudden detour to a village with his cousins confused him. Why did they need his presence now? Mo had lived in the States most of his life and his cousins had managed without him all that time, but Mark guessed it wasn't any of his business. The whole trip had turned out much differently that he had expected.

Why hadn't Mo spoken to anyone who wasn't a relative? At least, it seemed that way to Mark. Everyone they had met had been a cousin or an uncle or a close neighbor of one of them. Maybe Mo had spoken to them in Pashto and Mark just hadn't been aware, or when he hadn't been around, but if so, it seemed like Mo was relying on his memory as Mark hadn't seen any sign of a tape recorder. He was no expert writing a book, but he thought that it involved copious note-taking.

Sweat ran in rivulets down his back as he finished the last of the water he had brought with him. Thirst pushed thoughts of Mo from his mind and he focused on finding a drink. He started to pass a bazaar but with his water gone, he hoped that he would be able to find a refill there even though he'd learned the bazaars sold goods and not food.

At first, he didn't really pay attention to the goods on display, but after he found someone who showed him a well, Mark filled the bottle and then strolled along the stalls, sipping the water. One stall displayed a beautiful rug. He wasn't much of a decorator, but the artist in him appreciated the colors and patterns of the wool. The next stall had gorgeous scarves and he thought of his mother. She would love one and he figured he should get some kind of souvenir from his time here. He picked out one and paid for it, then realized he'd better get his dad something too.

He spotted a vendor with intricately carved wooden crafts. Perfect. His dad's hobby was working with wood. After looking over the selection, he chose a basket that collapsed. Not only was it very cool, he imagined his dad would find a use for the basket in his woodshed behind the house. It could hold nuts and screws or something. Satisfied with his purchases, he headed back to the road, but he passed a stall with a table full of old cameras. He could no more pass it by than a woman could pass a chocolate fountain.

Most of the cameras were relics and he picked up one, turning it over in his hands, smiling. His grandfather had owned one like it. He set it down, and scanned the rest. A few were only a decade or so out of date, but they were cheap models that he barely glanced at. He could find one of those in any thrift shop in the States. He saw a few models that he was pretty sure were Russian made and when he examined the back of one, the Cyrillic writing confirmed it. The camera was in good shape and he debated buying it. It had a big red '50' stamped on the top and he wondered what that meant. While he pondered its significance, his eyes wandered over the other cameras and caught on one. It didn't look very different from the Russian one, but the body had more metal and less plastic. He set the Russian camera down, the puzzle of the '50' forgotten. The air around the other camera seemed to shimmer. He cast a look over his shoulder at the setting sun. The rays must be hitting the table just right.

He picked up the camera and felt a jolt race up his arms and he lost his grip for a second, dropping it like a hot potato as he staggered back a few steps. Luckily, the camera only fell a few inches onto the table. He wiped his palms on his thighs. The vendor had started putting cameras away for the night and when he reached for the one Mark had dropped, a flash of irrational panic shot through him at the thought of losing it. He grabbed it before the vendor could. This time, there was no jolt, but there was...something. Like a thrum of energy. He could feel it run up his arms and wash over him.

It wasn't painful, but reminded him of one time when he was out in an electrical storm and the hair on his arms had stood on end just before lightening had struck a tree not more than a hundred feet from him. At the time, the lightning strike had terrified him, but later, he recalled the incredible energy that had enveloped him just before the bolt. It had been like being injected with a dozen cups of coffee, only that wasn't quite right. It wasn't a jittery feeling. It was as if someone had taken his nervous excitement from taking his first driver's exam or first kiss and mixed it with the burst of excitement he felt on Christmas mornings when he was still a kid and Santa was still very real.

He was at once filled with both confusion and assurance. His confusion came from not knowing the cause of the energy, but he was sure he had to have the camera. His gaze shot to the sky, certain he'd find a dark storm cloud above, but there was only a deepening blue sky that brightened to a brilliant orange in the west. The vendor didn't seem to notice anything amiss and had merely shrugged at Mark and put away a different camera.

Mark lifted the camera and tried to pantomime taking a photograph, asking, "Where did you get this? Does this work?"

Another shrug.

"Does that mean you don't know, or you just don't know what I'm asking?"

The vendor smiled and shook his head.

Mark decided it didn't matter if it worked. He had to have it. He rationalized that it would look great on a shelf in his studio if nothing else. He pulled out his wallet. "How much?"

At the sight of the wallet, the man knew exactly what Mark was asking and named his price. It was more than Mark expected, but he guessed he hadn't hid his eagerness very well. He was sure he could have haggled and bartered the price down, but he didn't want to take the time. After handing over the cash, he took the camera, surprised at the sense of calmness that washed over him once it was in his hands.

* * *

The next morning, he woke up early, eager to use the camera. He opened the back, searching for a source of the energy, but it appeared like any other camera. Disappointment swept through him, but then he felt silly. What had he expected? A tiny nuclear power plant churning inside? Despite the benign appearing interior, it was a very cool looking camera. He still felt the energy, but put it down to something he ate or maybe a virus he must have picked up. For all he knew, there were little parasites swimming in his blood right now. The thought made him shudder and drop the camera on the bed.

The energy stopped like someone had thrown a switch. If he had parasites, wouldn't they keep swimming or whatever they did until he either died or got rid of them? He reached out a finger and touched the camera. A sizzle of energy zoomed up his arm. He grinned. Parasites couldn't do that.

He wanted to use the camera, and while he hadn't found a nuclear power plant inside of it; he had found a lot of dust and sand. It was almost as if the thing had been buried in sand at one point, but luckily, the lens still retained its cap and he didn't detect any significant scratches. As much as he wanted to use it, he didn't want to ruin it, so he resigned himself to waiting until he was back in Chicago and could get it professionally cleaned.

With a sigh, he wrapped his softest t-shirt around it and packed it in his suitcase. He didn't have an extra camera bag and hoped it would be okay. Looking at it, he guessed it had to be about sixty years old and figured if it had made it this long in such good condition it should weather the trip to Chicago okay if he had it surrounded by his clothes.

His hotel had a shared bathroom with others on his floor, so he took his towel, washcloth and a clean t-shirt and boxers and tried to clean up the best he could in the tiny bathroom. Hopefully none of the other guests would need to use the facilities while he was busy.

He couldn't wait to get home and take a long, hot shower. He felt like he had dust embedded an inch deep in his pores and it would take months to feel clean again. Water was a commodity he had always taken for granted, but in his travels through Afghanistan, where it had to be drawn out of a well, he appreciated the effort it took to obtain it a lot more. The hotel had water, but the water pressure was a mere trickle and he filled up the basin and had to wash using that. Cupping the tepid water, he splashed his face, and then soaped up the washcloth, scrubbing his cheeks and his beard. There hadn't been many opportunities to look in a mirror the last few weeks and his appearance startled him. His skin was so brown and his beard longer than he had ever worn before. It was like looking at a stranger. Mentally, he added shaving to his 'To do' list when he returned. Feeling refreshed, if not exactly clean, he returned to his room to find Mo sitting on the only chair. If Mark had been dusty, Mo was positively filthy. And was that…blood on his neck?

"Mo? Are you okay? What the hell happened to you?"

"Nothing. My cousins and I camped out in the mountains with some other men from the village."

On one hand, Mark was a little disappointed that he hadn't been invited along. He and his dad used to camp and hunt when he was a kid. It might have been fun, but the prospect of camping with Faisal and Sayeed drained the appeal out of the idea. However, if Mo had asked him to go, he would have and done his best to avoid the cousins. Something of what he was feeling must have shown in his expression because Mo waved a hand dismissively.

"You wouldn't have liked it. It was more like a religious retreat than a camping trip. I would have told you about it before we left Chicago, but I wasn't sure if I would be able to go or not. They're very selective about who attends."

Mark shrugged and draped the damp towel over the doorknob, hoping it would dry before morning so he could use it again. "No problem. I spent my day exploring Kabul and found the coolest old camera at a bazaar. I've packed it already, but give me a second and I'll show it to you."

Mo shook his head. "Sorry, maybe later. My room's next door and I need to hit the bed hard."

His enthusiasm faltered, but Mark nodded. "Sure. I'll see you in the morning."

CHAPTER THREE

The loft was cool from the air conditioner, but even with it running full blast, it couldn't erase all of the humidity from the Chicago air. With trepidation, Mark unwrapped the camera, freeing it from the confines of the t-shirt. What if he had only imagined the energy? Or what it had just been some kind of strange static electricity from the hot, dry air in Afghanistan? He had been back home for five days already, but he had been so busy catching up on photography shoots, paying bills, and processing the photos he had taken in Afghanistan, that he hadn't had a moment to play with the camera.

A frisson of excitement hit him as his fingers brushed the metal and energy raced up his arms. "Yes!" He set out the soft brushes he had taken from his studio. He wasn't sure he wanted to trust the camera to anyone else to clean. What if they did something and it lost the energy? He couldn't explain why it was so important to him, just that it felt right. Without it, it would be nothing but a pretty showpiece. Nice, but not very exciting.

He put on some music and spent the rest of the evening cleaning every nook and cranny of the camera, using a can of compressed air to get the sand and dust out of cracks he couldn't reach with his brushes.

Satisfied at last, he stretched and glanced at the clock. Tomorrow was Saturday and other than a quick headshot for a kid in the morning, he didn't have anything else

M.P. McDonald

scheduled. He would try out the camera the next
afternoon. It looked like standard 35mm film would work.
The source of the energy became an even bigger puzzle to
him because there was no obvious source. Everything on
the device was mechanical, not electrical.

Saturday morning couldn't pass fast enough. The kid
had been cute and mostly cooperative so Mark had
recommended a couple of agents to the mom. Something
about the boy reminded him of the little boy in
Afghanistan. Maybe it was just his dark hair and eyes, but
Mark took it as a good sign for trying out the camera.
Maybe it was a sign that the camera would work.

Finally. Mark strolled along the lakefront, enjoying
the great weather and taking shots of whatever caught his
eye. Tufts of grass sprouting from sand dunes, the lake,
and he even sprawled on the ground and took a photo
straight up through the leaves of a tree. He thought it
might show some good contrast between the dark leaves
and the dapple of sunlight. The lake was choppy and kids
stood in front of the waves, squealing and laughing as the
waves carried them in to shore. He sat on the beach and
drew his arm over his brow. The sun beat down and the
water looked inviting. Too bad he hadn't thought to wear
his swimming trunks.

A few women in bikinis were lying on the sand and
he couldn't help contrasting their mode of dress with what
he had seen in Afghanistan. He had never thought twice
about a woman in a swimsuit except to enjoy the view.
When that thought hit him, he felt added heat creep up his
neck. Were women there forced to wear the suffocating
burqas to protect them from guys like him who had
indecent thoughts about women in bikinis? He shook off
the idea. It wasn't like he acted on the thoughts. The more

42

he contemplated the burqas and their use, the more insulted he became. He had self-control; it wasn't as if he was going to throw the nearest woman in a bikini down in the sand and have his way with her, but the dress restrictions seemed to imply that men couldn't control themselves.

At that moment, the woman turned her head and opened her eyes. A smile tugged at the corner of her mouth as her eyes met his. He blinked and turned away, embarrassed to be caught staring, and the heat turned to a burning flame of embarrassment. If she only knew what he had been thinking...Mark looked again, feeling the urge to explain, but she had closed her eyes again. Obviously his attention hadn't disturbed her. He stood and brushed sand off his pants and headed for home.

* * *

Mark had a darkroom in his studio, but only used it occasionally when he wanted a special effect. It was more cost-effective to send his film into a company to get developed and get proof sheets. It allowed him to book more shoots if he didn't have to spend a lot of time developing film, but sometimes he missed doing his own, so he took the opportunity to develop the film from his first use of the antique camera in his own studio. When he had finished and they were dry enough to handle, he sorted through them.

The tuft of grass and the tree photos turned out pretty cool, but the one of the lake was flat. Mark frowned and set it aside. He should have focused on something on the lake such as a sailboat. Disappointment at the ordinary photos drained some of his excitement. For some reason, he had expected more, but the reality was, it was an old camera and the device was only as good as its operator. He stared at the picture of the water and shook his head. Boring. What had he been thinking? He tossed it aside. The second to last photo stopped him cold.

A little girl was sprawled on the sand and what appeared to be a lifeguard was pinching her nose as he leaned over her. His other hand tilted her chin and it was apparent he had either just given her a breath or was about to give one. A woman had a hand on the child's chest, and her face was contorted with anguish. He stared, trying to comprehend where the photo had come from. He had put his own film in. He was mystified. Had he somehow clicked the shutter by accident and taken the picture? It didn't make sense. Maybe there was some way the film could have been packaged with this photo already on it. He didn't know how, but it was the only explanation he could come up with. The little girl's eyes were open just a fraction, and he shuddered at the blank stare.

The last photo was one he had taken of a kite in the sky. It was okay, but it added to his confusion about the image of the little girl. He would expect something like that to be on end of the film, otherwise he would have had a double exposure with his own photo superimposed over the one of the little girl, but he saw no evidence of that. If it had been at the end, he could see where he had thought the film was finished, maybe the counter was off or something.

Mark blew out a deep breath and flipped through the photos again. It didn't make any more sense the second time through, so he tried to put it out of his mind and when his friend George Ortega called to see if he wanted to go out for a few beers and a game of pool, he jumped at the offer.

He sipped his beer and leaned against the bar as George lined up a shot, but all he could see was the little girl lying in the sand.

"Hello?"

Blinking, Mark flinched as George waved a hand in front of Mark's face. Annoyed, Mark said, "What?"

"Dude. It's your turn."

The annoyance slipped away. "Sorry, man. I was just thinking about something."

"No problem." George held up his bottle of beer. "You ready for another?"

Tilting his bottle, Mark drained it and shook his head. "No, I think I'm going to finish this game and then head out."

George glanced at his watch and shook his head in disbelief. "It's not even ten yet. Man, you're getting old!" A smile took the edge off the dig. He set his bottle down. "Then we might as well finish up before I get a refill."

Obliging, Mark took his shot and made it, but missed the next one. George ran the table after that.

Mark returned the cue to the wall holder and shook George's hand. "You finally got me. I'll bring my 'A' game next week. You better watch out."

With a laugh, George shook his head. "I might quit while I'm ahead. Whatever it was distracting you tonight worked out in my favor."

He was about to deny the distraction, but shrugged instead. "Yeah. Sorry about that. I was a little preoccupied."

"Hey, how did it go in Afghanistan? I heard you and Mo went there?"

Mark dug in his pocket for his car keys, spinning them around his finger as he replied, "It went...okay. It didn't go quite as I planned though."

Leaning against the bar, George signaled for another beer. "Really? What happened?"

Mark was tempted to tell George about Mo's lack of contribution towards taking the photos for the book, but he thought better of it. It wasn't like Mark had been overworked, and it was possible Mo had always intended for Mark to do most of the photography while he supplied the narrative. Besides, it was Mo's book and he had paid for Mark's trip so he wasn't out anything except a few weeks' time. "Nothing I can put my finger on. I probably misunderstood what my role was; besides I got a cool looking antique camera from a bazaar. So in the end, it was all good. Anyway, I'll see ya later. "

George clapped him on the back. "Later, amigo."

* * *

At home, Mark eyed the stack of photos he had left on the coffee table and couldn't resist sorting through them until he found the one of the little girl again. He studied it for several minutes, noticing the features of the lifeguard for the first time. He looked vaguely familiar. Had he been working the beach where Mark had taken the photos of the lake? It was hard to tell because he had only seen the young man at a distance but the dark hair was right. If it was the same guy, he certainly hadn't been performing CPR when Mark had spotted him.

A throbbing headache took up residence behind his eyes and he let the picture slide from his fingers to rub his temples. There was no explanation for the picture. At least nothing that made sense. He headed to bed, detouring to the sink for a glass of water and a couple of aspirin.

The little girl played in the surf, her squeals of delight nearly drowned out by the pounding waves. Her mother stood in the water nearby, watching with an indulgent smile. A young boy called to her and she turned away and spoke to him, saying something about a cooler. When she returned her attention to her daughter, the little girl was gone. The mother's scream pierced the air. Mark stood on the edge of the shore wanting to dive in to search, but his feet felt mired in the sand. He struggled to lift them to no avail. A dark haired young man in red swimming trunks rushed past and dove into the water. The mother kept pointing to the last place she had seen her daughter and screaming, "Gabby!"

Another lifeguard, a woman, joined the first. A third must have signaled to the rest of the swimmers to leave the water, because soon the beach was full of children, but a hush had fallen. Sirens wailed in the distance. An eternity passed before the male lifeguard emerged from the water with the little girl limp in his arms. He was already giving mouth to mouth. The female lifeguard took the girl and set her on the sand as she checked for a pulse. Mark flinched when his gaze reached the little girl's eyes. They were open, but flat and unmoving. Like a porcelain doll, she stared at the sky.

The duo performed CPR until paramedics arrived. The paramedics took over CPR with a third paramedic trying to start an I.V. He shook his head and then reached into his box for something and a minute later, to Mark's horror, pushed something into the little girl's leg just below the knee. His stomach flipped and he broke out in a cold sweat.

Mark jolted awake with a gasp. Levering up on his elbows, he cast a wild look around the room, blinking in surprise when he found he was in bed and not standing on the beach. *A dream! Thank god.* A whiff of fish and lake water followed him from his dream, but even as he recognized the scent, it slipped away. He flopped back and scrubbed his hands down his face. His heart hammering and wide awake now, he sat on the edge of the bed. His palms rested on his thighs, but they shook like a china plate in an earthquake. Unsettled, he stood and went to the kitchen for a drink of water. He gulped down a full glass, finally ridding his mouth of the gritty foul taste before he went into the living room area and turned on a light. The photos still sat on the coffee table. He ignored them and wished he had never seen the picture of the little girl. He guessed it must have been on his mind as he fell asleep and the image had entered his dream, turning from a still photo to a full featured film.

His imagination had even added details like the fishy smell and the little girl's name. Where had he come up with that one? He didn't know any Gabbys. He sank onto the sofa, his mind going over the dream until he finally became drowsy again, and turned to lie on the couch, pulling the blanket folded on the back down over him.

He slept until his phone woke him up and he bolted out of bed again. He found his phone on the kitchen counter and recognized Mo's number on the caller ID. "Hello?"

"Hey, Mark. Did I wake you?"

Mark glanced at the clock on the stove. Seven-thirty a.m. "Uh, no, not really. I needed to get out of bed anyway. So…what's up?"

"I got your film sorted out from the trip and you have some great shots. I'll be going through them and matching them up to points I'll be making in the book. I just wondered if you could go over some of them with me and give me the background on them. I didn't realize you had taken so many photos."

Mark scratched his head and yawned. With his brain still foggy from sleep it took him a second to get his bearings. Today was Sunday and he had nothing booked. "Sure, no problem. I can be there about ten."

"Sounds good."

As soon as Mark hung up, he regretted his promise to go, which puzzled him. He stumbled back to the couch and grabbed the blanket, wrapping it over his shoulders as he curled on his side. Since they had returned from Afghanistan, he hadn't heard from Mo. Something had been off about the last part of the trip—Mo had not only gone on a retreat, but had retreated into himself, barely speaking to him during the long return flight. Mark had tried to put it off to fatigue, but he couldn't help wondering if he had offended Mo's family somehow. Granted, he *had* taken photos of women, but after the one time he had been caught, he had been careful and had refrained from even glancing at a woman. Most of his photos had been taken with his telephoto lens to minimize the chance that anyone would know exactly what he was photographing.

Mark let the blanket slide off his shoulders and headed for the shower. Even though he had looked forward to working on the book, he was reluctant to do it today. Instead, the urge to return to the beach where he had taken the photos with the old camera gnawed at him, but he had no rational reason to go back. It wasn't like the

49

little girl would be lying there in the sand. It had just been a dream provoked no doubt by the crazy photos. Besides, he wanted to find out if he had done something to anger Mo.

* * *

"Good morning, Mo," Mark said as his friend waved him into his apartment. "I brought some coffee and donuts." He raised a bag of donuts for his friend to see and balanced a cardboard tray with the coffee cups and an assortment of creamers in his other hand.

"Thanks. Just set it on the kitchen table. Be careful of the papers and photos though."

Mark complied, angling his head to see the picture peeking out from beneath the papers. It was the blue color that had caught his eye. It was the color of many of the burqas that the women in Afghanistan had worn. He had seen a few other colors like black or gray, but blue had been the most common color.

He started to reach for the photo, but Mo grabbed his arm. "Hold on. I have them numbered and stuff. I don't want to mess it up."

"Sorry." He tried not to take offense at the reprimand, but there was something about Mo's tone that bugged him. Taking a coffee from the tray, he shrugged off the annoyance and peeled the plastic tab back on the lid. Ignoring the creamers — they were for Mo, he took a sip. Maybe his own feeling of anxiety about his dream and his irritation with Mo was simply a lack of caffeine.

"So how does this all work?"

Mo shrugged. "I have a few connections. In fact, our trip was paid for by a sponsor."

"Really?" Mark grinned. It had bothered him that his friend had paid for the tickets and accommodations, such as they were, but he reminded himself that he hadn't been paid for his work while over there either and he had taken time from his own business to go. "Who's the sponsor? A women's organization?" It made sense to him.

Instead of answering, Mo narrowed his eyes. "It doesn't concern you."

Taken aback, Mark set his coffee down and spread his hands. "Did I piss you off somehow?"

The hostile look dropped off Mo's face and although a smile replaced it, it didn't quite reach his eyes. "No. I just have a lot on my mind."

"Look, I've got a lot on my mind today too, so why don't we do this another time?"

"But you might forget the details."

Thinking back to the circumstances surrounding the photos, Mark shook his head. "No way."

Mo scowled, made a shooing motion and said, "Then go. I know this means nothing to you. I might just throw all your photos away."

Stunned at the reaction, Mark remained rooted to the kitchen floor for a moment, but then spun for the door ready to slam it on his way out, but instead, he stopped with his hand on the knob and turned to face Mo. "You know, I was honored when you asked me to go to Afghanistan with you. It was an opportunity to do some good and I wanted to be a part of it, but I have to admit that I was also eager to get my photos in your book." His face heated at the admission as he avoided Mo's eyes. "Most of my jobs are ads in magazines or catalogs. Basically, my photos *sell* stuff. That wasn't how I envisioned my career when I started out. I looked at this as my big chance to make an impression—you know, like those iconic photos in *Life* or *Time*."

He paused and blew out a deep breath as he tried to put into words the frustration he felt, his hand tightening on the knob. "But after seeing that woman beaten, it just seemed like I wasn't able to do enough—that I won't ever be able to do enough—but I still gotta try. So, you do whatever you want to do with the photos, but you are dead wrong when you said the book meant nothing to me."

The anger had eased from Mo's expression, but he remained silent.

With a firm nod, Mark left, pulling the door closed behind him with a soft click.

* * *

"Dammit!"

Mark banged his fist on the steering wheel after starting his Jeep. He glared at the apartment building, debating if he should go back in and finish detailing the photographs. His stomach rumbled and he realized he never had eaten a donut. *To hell with it*. He would give it a week and call Mo. By then this would all blow over.

He drove aimlessly, but before he knew it, he was at the same beach he had been at yesterday. He felt silly chasing after the nightmare and chided himself that it had been nothing, just a bad dream. Anxiety still churned in his gut, but he blamed it on hunger. Following that logic, he grabbed a burger at a drive through and headed back to the loft to watch a Cub's game.

As he dozed on the sofa, remnants of last night's dream plagued his sleep. The details weren't as clear as they had been during the night, but that fact didn't ease his anxiety, and instead only fed it. As the images blurred, he awoke to a feeling of overwhelming despair. He sat on edge of the sofa, head bent, massaging the back of his neck. This was crazy. He stood and paced to the window, bracing his hands against the side window. He had never been plagued by nightmares before. In fact, he couldn't remember the last time he'd had one. Maybe when he was six or seven? So why now?

Brimming with questions but void of answers he could think of only one way to get rid of the image once and for all. He had to go to the beach and prove to whatever inner demon was harassing him that there was no little girl drowning on the beach.

* * *

It was after three when he arrived. Parking had been almost impossible to obtain and now, hot and sweaty, he strode along the shore, photo in hand as he tried to match up the images in it to any of the beachgoers. With such a hot day and back to school just around the corner, the beach was packed.

At first, Mark tried to match up the little girls running around and splashing in the surf with the image of the little girl in his photo, but the child in the picture was so lifeless, she didn't seem to resemble any of the children he could see. As he stalked back and forth along the shore, he attempted to locate where on the lengthy beach the CPR scene had taken place. In the background of the photo, he saw pilings in the water, but that didn't help pinpoint the site because they occurred at regular intervals a few hundred feet from shore. The back of his neck burned from the sun, but even worse, he felt the blistering stares of some of the parents. He couldn't blame them for being suspicious. If he ever had a kid, he would be keeping a sharp eye on any guy who behaved as he was.

The crowd finally started to thin out as families packed up and parents took their tired children home. Mark felt stupid as he trudged through the sand on his third pass along the shore. Kids were starting to look familiar now, but he didn't know if it was because of the photo or only because he had seen them on his first two passes. He scanned the water, but after an hour, the glare from the water sent a spike of pain through his forehead and he longed to go home. He would just go to the end one more time, turn around and walk back.

Halfway to the end, he spotted a girl whose swimsuit resembled the one on the girl in the photo, but she was only knee deep and scooped water in a little cup, dumped it and repeated the process several times. She seemed fascinated with pouring the water through the fingers of her opposite hand. Mark smiled and continued to the far end of the beach, did an about face and headed back. When he was at the mid-point, he looked for the little girl again. A shard of fear cut into him. He couldn't see her, but he brushed his fear aside. The assurance acted as a Band-Aid as he tried to stifle his irrational fear. She had only been a few steps into the water, and her mother had probably just called her back to their blanket or something. This whole exercise had been a waste of time on his part, but at least now he could put the nightmare to bed.

A scream rent the air and an instant later, the lifeguard's whistle blew. Mark felt as if someone had slugged him in the chest and zapped him with a Taser all at the same time. He spun and watched as a lifeguard dove into a wave. A woman sobbed and pointed into the water as a lifeguard from an adjacent chair raced to the point where the first had gone in. The lifeguard blew her whistle and directed everyone to get out of the water.

The first lifeguard surfaced much farther out than Mark would have expected in such a short time, but the young man only came up briefly, grabbed a breath of air and ducked beneath the surf. He repeated the process several times before he came up with a limp little girl. She was the same girl that he had passed just moments before.

Horror lodged in Mark's throat, choking him. He staggered back as the lifeguard laid the little girl upon the packed sand. Mark gulped in an attempt to swallow the horror. *Her eyes.* Merely slits and absent signs of life, they reflected only blue sky. With a hoarse curse, he stumbled and turned, racing for his car. How could he have taken this picture *yesterday?* At the bottom of a dune, his knees gave out and he vomited onto a tuft of grass.

* * *

Mark glared at the picture, pointing with one finger as he kept a tight grip on the neck of a beer bottle.

"You can't exist!"

With a sharp flick of his wrist, he tried to send the photo sailing across the room, but it boomeranged and landed on the recliner to his right. The little girl was head down, and from this angle, the slit eyes seemed to watch his every move. Upside down, the photo appeared sinister, her eyes accusing him of failing to save her.

"I didn't know! I didn't *know*...how was I supposed to *know* you were real?"

He drowned a sob, tipped the beer bottle, and drained it. Leaning forward, he set it on the coffee table, not caring when it wobbled and fell, rolling into the six other bottles before stopping with a clink.

His phone rang and he glanced over to where it rested on the cushion beside him. *Mo.* He didn't pick it up and instead, opened a fresh beer from the carton. He had five more. That should be enough to get him some sleep without the nightmare of the drowned little girl.

He flipped the beer cap, aiming for the now empty carton of the recently polished off six-pack, but missed and the cap skittered off the table and rolled in a circle before spinning to a stop beneath the chair. He took a long noisy guzzle, lowering the bottle and wiping his mouth with the back of his hand. *Why* had he been shown the tragedy? *And how?* He didn't believe in psychics or telepathy or any of that crazy hocus pocus shit. When he had arrived home, he had opened the back of the camera, inspecting the inside. There was absolutely nothing within it which could explain how it could have worked. It was just an old scratched hunk of metal.

Whatever the method of showing the future, it was clear the method worked. It had shown him a dead kid and that was exactly what he had seen the next day. Was it some kind of cruel punishment from…from whatever had imparted the magic into the camera? Magic! That was it. The camera was magic. If he couldn't figure it out he would assume it was magic. He nodded, ignoring the dizziness the movement caused, and took another drink. Satisfied with the source of the power, he no longer cared how it came to be in the camera. It could have been God or aliens, or hell, it could have been a young boy wizard.

What had he done to piss off an alien? Why him? The camera was from Afghanistan and he had only tried to help the Afghani women. It didn't seem fair. Shame flooded him, sloshing around in his veins with the blood and alcohol. Why *not* him? Here he was whining about fairness when he was just fine and dandy, all the while that sweet little girl was dead. No wonder he was being punished. All he would have had to do was keep an eye on her. He could have saved her if he had tried, but instead, he had walked past, even knowing that she resembled the girl in his picture. But he hadn't really been looking for a live girl. He had been looking for a dead one, and eventually, he'd found her.

With a choked cry, he threw the half-full bottle against the column of brick that made up the opposite wall. Beer and glass exploded in the room. Sitting on the edge of the couch with his elbows braced on his knees, he covered his face.

Emotionally drained, he slumped back but didn't reach for another beer. What if he had stayed near the child? Could he really have saved her? It didn't seem possible. Even if the camera was magical and could photograph the future, how could that future be changed? Wouldn't the act of changing it render the photograph impossible? Wasn't that some kind of paradox or something? His brain was muddled with alcohol, but he was sure there was something about paradoxes in *Back to the Future*. Marty couldn't interfere too much or it would alter the future in unpredictable ways. He shook his head in wry disgust that he was basing his camera's magical properties on Hollywood science. What the hell, it made as much sense as anything else he could come up with.

What if he tested his hypothesis about the camera being magical? He could take some more pictures and see if any showed the future. He jumped off the couch, staggering just a little as he strode to the kitchen counter and grabbed the camera. He had some film in his camera bag and he loaded it. There was just enough light to get a few pictures if he hurried.

Flinging open a window, he took random photos of the street below. He didn't care about composition or lighting, he just aimed and clicked on pedestrians crossing the street, a truck double-parked, a dog trotting down the street, and more until the roll was finished.

As he developed the film, it dawned on him that what he was doing could be considered borderline crazy and if he told anyone, they would laugh their asses off, and then call the men in the white coats. What sane person took photos with the expectation that some of them might be photos of the future?

For the most part, the resulting photos appeared to be exactly as he photographed them, except for one. He was sure he had taken a few pictures of a double-parked truck near the intersection, but instead of the truck, he had two images that he didn't recall taking. He should have taken notes so he would know exactly what he had photographed, but it was too late now. He would have to rely on memory. The sedan was parked at the curb in one photo. A man was in the driver's seat and from the angle of the wheels and the way he was looking at his side-view mirror, he appeared to be pulling away from the curb. In the second photo, the car was crushed in the intersection by a beer truck. There was no doubt he would have remembered taking a photograph of that if it had happened.

Mark studied the two photographs of the sedan, setting them on the kitchen counter as he rubbed the back of his neck and thought back to the photo with the child. Were there clues in it that he could have used to save her? Since he had taken the photo straight down, he couldn't determine the angle of the sun. While it was evening now, did that correspond to when the accident would take place? Would it happen tomorrow, next week or fifteen minutes from now? The possibilities were endless and they churned through his mind like a locomotive with each boxcar representing another scenario.

He noted the white box truck behind the sedan. There was writing on the side; that in itself was a clue, as most were painted with the name of a business. Rummaging in his junk drawer, he found a small flip notepad and jotted down the white truck clue. Obviously the sedan itself was the biggest clue. He could watch for that car and when it showed up, warn the driver and—what was he thinking? He threw the pencil down in frustration. Nobody would believe him. He could hear himself now…'Uh, excuse me, but when you leave the curb, you're going to get clocked in the intersection.' Should he show the photo to the man? He played that over in his imagination and couldn't see it ending well. The man would think he was a nut right out of the *Twilight Zone*. Which brought up another worry— even if for some bizarre reason the man did believe him, where did that leave the man? Would he ever be able to pull the car from the curb or would there always be a beer truck in its future? What if the sedan was towed? Would that action save the car and the driver or place the tow truck in jeopardy too? He fought the urge to toss the photos in the trash and instead, slammed a fist on the counter and stabbed both hands through his hair.

His head pounded with tension and he finally gave up running all the different scenarios over in his mind, took a couple of pain relievers and went to bed.

* * *

In the morning, he woke up, pulled on yesterday's jeans, shoved his feet into his sneakers and grabbed a butcher knife out of his kitchen drawer. He knew he looked like a demented psychopath as he raced down the steps, but he had dreamed of the photo. The man was going into the bakery across the street. Mark had seen him in the dream. He came out with a white bag and a cup of coffee that he sipped before opening the car door. His attire had been business, but most importantly, Mark had felt like he had been in the car when the man had started it. He distinctly heard the deejay on the radio say the time. When he had awakened, it was only five minutes before that time.

His only hope was to disable the vehicle. Speaking to the impending victim was too unpredictable. The guy would in all likelihood ignore the warning. Mark knew he would if put in the man's shoes. Just before he awoke, his dream self was getting a knife, and so he did the same. He could puncture the tires and prevent the car from being driven.

He burst through the door to the outside, and leaped down the five steps from the stoop. He stumbled a step before regaining his balance and dodged a passing car, ignoring the blast of its horn. With a glance left and right, Mark jabbed the knife several times into the front driver's side wheel. No way the man would miss it, but for good measure, he did the same to the back wheel. He prayed the tires would go flat before the car left the curb. The accident happened only a few hundred feet up the road, so if the tires weren't noticeably flat, the man might drive off anyway and still get demolished.

Chest heaving, Mark took a step back and listened to the hiss of air escaping the tires. The sound reassured him but before he had time to congratulate his ingenuity, the owner of the car exited the bakery.

"*Hey!* What are you doing?" The man's steps quickened as he rounded the back of his car.

Mark bolted back across the street and circled to the back of his own building, and didn't stop until he was on the next block over. As he passed a Dumpster, he tossed the knife inside and eased his head around the corner to the sidewalk. Head cocked, he listened for sirens — either from the man reporting him or from someone reporting an accident.

He walked another six blocks in the opposite direction, worried that any moment a cop car would pull alongside the curb and arrest him. Geez, he was acting like an escaped murderer. He needed to just chill and get a grip on his nerves. When no cop car approached, he finally felt safe in heading back. Ambling along with his hands shoved in his pockets, he hoped he looked innocent, but he felt like he had the word 'Vandal' taped on front of his shirt like a nametag.

It had been about twenty minutes and when a tow truck passed him and stopped near where he thought the car had been parked, he let out a breath of relief. He hid in the alcove of an art supply store for a little while longer, allowing the tow truck time to haul the vehicle away.

When the coast was clear, he returned to his apartment and found the photographs on his kitchen counter still, only now they showed a double-parked truck—the very same one that had been in that spot last night.

With a whoop, he pumped his fist in the air. He had done it! He had changed the photo. His cheeks felt like they were going to split from the strain of his grin. Would the driver even know that Mark had saved his life? For a second, he felt a sense of loss. It would have been nice to have a little recognition, but in his dream, he had seen a car seat in the back of the car along with a few small toys. The man was a father—Mark was sure of it—and now he wouldn't leave his child fatherless. That was worth it even if he was the only one who would ever know it.

* * *

After that first incredible save, Mark couldn't resist using the camera every day. It was never a given that he would get a future photo, but that was half the draw. Some days, he developed the exact same photos that he had taken, but other days, a photo that didn't belong would show up—sometimes more than one of the same incident. After studying the photos in the evening, he'd sleep, and the photos would come to life in his dreams. Day after day, he took the photos, and day after day, he made the saves. Like notches on a gun belt, he kept track, saving the photos of the ones he'd changed in a box under his bed. Someday maybe he'd tell someone about the camera, but for now, he kept it to himself. It wasn't that he didn't want to share the secret—he did. The desire to tell someone was always coiled inside of him, ready to spring out, but as badly as he wanted to tell someone, he didn't dare. What if someone stole it? He couldn't bear to lose it, but he was sure that if news got out, it would be a target for theft. Who wouldn't want a camera that showed the future?

Another fear was, even if he gave in to the temptation to show someone else, what if it didn't work when he tried to demonstrate the power? He would look like a fool. His greatest fear was that the government would get a hold of it. He knew what they would do. They would tear it apart to find out how it worked. It would be studied and tested and meanwhile, people who might have been saved would die while they ran their damn tests. Nope. Sharing the secret wasn't an option. At least not at this time.

About nine months after the first save, Mark sat on the edge of his bed and studied the latest photograph. It showed a clerk at a gas station in the process of being robbed at gunpoint. In the next photo, the clerk was on the floor behind the counter in a puddle of blood. He had taken the pictures the day before and the corresponding dream was still fresh in his mind. Taking his notes with him, he moved into the kitchen and sat on the stool at the breakfast bar.

So far, most of his saves had involved accidents, not crimes. Could he prevent this? And if so, how? He didn't own a gun and even if he did, he wasn't about to get in a gunfight. He would probably do more damage than the criminal. No, he would have to notify the police about it. Somehow. His first challenge was nailing down the precinct where the robbery would take place. He pulled out the phone book and looked up the addresses, and picked out the precincts closest to the gas station. He stared at the numbers on the pad of paper, tapping the end of his pen against the pad. Now what? Just call them and report a robbery before it happened? They would either think he was involved or that he was a nutcase. The dream image of the murdered clerk popped into his mind's eye. He would have to risk it. Better to be thought a nutcase than to carry the guilt of doing nothing and letting the woman die.

He called a precinct and tried to explain that he had overheard some man planning a robbery, but the person he spoke to transferred him to a detective. Just great. He had planned on delivering the tip to some random dispatcher.

"Detective Bishop speaking."

"Uh, yeah—", he broke off and cleared his throat. He hadn't counted on speaking with a detective and wondered if he should just hang up and try to take care of it himself. His story was thin and wouldn't hold up under close scrutiny.

"I uh, I want to report a conversation that I overheard this morning. A guy was planning to rob a gas station at Lake Street and North Green."

"Really?" The skepticism crackled through the line and almost bit him in the ear.

He shook off the nerves and kept his voice firm. "Yes, *really*."

"Where were you when you overhead the conversation?"

"I was...I was at a bar."

"What bar?"

His mind went blank. "Just some bar over on...on Division."

"What block on Division?"

Mark stifled a groan of frustration. "I don't know. Just a place on West Division."

She sighed. "You don't sound too sure of yourself. Were you drinking at the time?"

"Sure, I'd had a beer, but I wasn't drunk if that's what you're asking." Denying drinking would be suspicious, so he felt clever admitting to a beer.

"Okay. Well, give me the details. Time? A description of the person?"

Relieved to have the answers to these questions, he rattled off information on the man in the picture, right down to the brand of shoes he was wearing.

"You noticed his *shoes*?"

"Well...yeah. Once I heard the plan, I tried to take note of as much as I could to pass along." He took a sip of his coffee, his mouth suddenly dry.

"And this guy just stood there while you took notes?" She was smirking. He couldn't see it but he could hear it. "Maybe you should have just taken a picture—it might have been less obvious."

Mark inhaled the hot coffee and coughed uncontrollably while he held his hand over the receiver.

"Hello? Are you all right?"

"Yeah, sorry. Coffee went down the wrong pipe." A lingering cough punctuated his reply.

"Okay, and your name?"

"What? My name? Why? I would prefer to give the tip anonymously."

"I need it for the report. I could take it anonymously, but we don't have time to run around checking out bogus reports and anonymous reports could come from a criminal looking for a diversion. " Any concern that might have been in her voice had evaporated and replaced with suspicion. "Is that what you're doing? Creating a diversion?"

"No, of course not."

"You got something to hide?"

If only she knew. He took a deep breath. "Mark Taylor." Resigned, he gave her his address and other details then said, "So you guys will stop it, right?"

"Listen, Mr. Taylor, if this information has a shred of truth to it, we'll find out and stop the robbery, but if you're yanking our chain, you are going to be in a world of hurt."

"No...I'm not...I'm not yanking your chain." He ran a hand through his hair then bit back a curse when his knee bumped against the bottom of the breakfast bar.

* * *

At the time of the robbery, Mark stood on the corner outside the gas station pretending to wait for a bus, but ready to do what he could if the police didn't show. When the bus stopped, he waved it off, ignoring the bus driver's irritated shake of his head.

Where were the cops? Any minute the robber would show up. Not five seconds later, a man matching the image in Mark's photo stepped out of a car, looked around and entered the gas station.

Mark jogged across the gas station lot, but as he reached for the door, two cop cars barreled into the lot. He halted and backed away from the door. A dark sedan followed the marked cars and he was pretty sure it was the detective. He hoped that meant they had been watching. The way the police cars were parked, the robber wouldn't be able to get away. One officer pressed his shoulder microphone as he read the numbers off the license plate aloud, and Mark glanced through the window, catching a glimpse of the robber. So far, he was only standing in the back, holding a cooler open, a soft drink in hand, but his attention was on the police cars outside. His gaze swung towards Mark, so Mark ducked out of the way, deciding that the police had things under control and didn't need him getting in the way. He retreated to the other side of the street where he could watch without attracting notice.

It seemed to take forever, but the police finally exited with the guy in handcuffs. Puzzled, Mark wondered what had happened to produce that result. He was sure no shots had been fired. Still, his plan had worked. Maybe he hadn't done it himself, but the end result was all that mattered. He took a deep breath and blew it out in relief. The robbery had been averted.

The next day, he was at his desk preparing to send out contact sheets to some clients, when the phone rang.

"Mark Taylor Photography." He sealed the envelope in his hand and tossed it on the desk, then reached for another client's contact sheet.

"Hello. This is Detective Bishop. We spoke yesterday."

He stilled with his hand poised over the contact sheet, his task forgotten for the moment. After observing the arrest, he had been confident that everything had come out okay. What if he had been wrong and the clerk had been murdered anyway? "I...uh...I hope my information helped."

"That's the thing. It did help, but it also means I'd like to ask you a few questions regarding how you acquired the information."

"Am I in trouble?"

"Not necessarily. I'm just curious because the guy we booked swears he wasn't in any bar on Division in the recent past. In fact, he claims he never spoke of his intentions to anyone and that the robbery was a spur of the moment thing."

Caught flat-footed, Mark could only stare across the office at framed photographs of a few Chicago celebrities. "Oh." Brilliant.

"I'd like to keep this unofficial, and if you have a satisfactory answer, we'll drop it but if you don't cooperate, we may have to go through official channels."

"Okay." As if he had a choice.

"I'm about to go for lunch now, so why don't you meet me?"

Although phrased as a suggestion or request, Mark wasn't fooled. It was an order. "I can do that. Where should we meet?"

"The burger place on the corner of Ohio and LaSalle. What do you look like?"

"Excuse me?"

"I doubt we'll be the only two people in the restaurant and I'd rather not ask every man there if he's Mark Taylor."

"Right. Well, I'm about six-one, dark hair." He glanced down. "And I'm wearing a dark blue polo shirt and jeans." He was going to ask what she looked like, but thought better of it. She was a detective and this was her idea, so she would have to find him, not the other way around.

"Okay, not the most detailed, but it'll do. I'll find you."

* * *

Mark set his cup of coffee on the stainless steel counter and peeled off the lid. He was hungry, but decided to wait to eat. It wasn't like she had actually invited him to eat with her, and it would be awkward if he already had a meal, so he ordered a coffee. He couldn't go wrong with that. Taking a sip, he turned to find who could only be Detective Bishop a few feet away. Something about her demeanor made him think she had been watching him, but she approached as soon as he made eye contact.

"Mr. Taylor?"

Mark transferred the cup to his left hand and extended his right. "Detective Bishop. Yes, I'm Mark."

Her blond hair was pulled back into a tight bun, and she didn't crack a smile, so he was surprised that her hand felt soft and warm in his. For some reason, he expected it to be firm and cold, like her attitude. She wore dark slacks and a white blouse with a blazer that matched her pants, but despite the plain attire, she couldn't hide her trim figure. Mark tried not to stare.

"Mark," she glanced over her shoulder at the counter, "why don't you grab a seat while I to go order." She started to turn, but then faced him again. "Have you eaten yet?"

Lifting his cup, Mark said, "No, but I'm good."

She nodded and took a place in line. Mark found a seat facing the front of the restaurant. With her back turned, he didn't even have to pretend he wasn't staring. The back view was as appealing as the front, but he shook off his impure thoughts. She was a cop, for crying out loud. A cop who wanted to question him.

She returned carrying a tray bearing her lunch of a cheeseburger, small fries and a large drink. Sitting, she shrugged out of the blazer and twisted to drape it over the back of her chair. More impure thoughts crossed his mind at her profile, but the holster strapped over her shoulder, and the butt of the gun under her left arm banished the thoughts almost immediately. The badge clipped to her belt didn't hurt either.

He sipped his coffee, unsure what to say, and decided to let her do all the talking. Maybe if he kept his mouth shut he could climb out of this hole of suspicion he had fallen into.

She washed down the first bite with a sip of pop, then said, "So, what's the deal? I can't figure out how you knew someone was going to rob that gas station at that time. Either you had inside knowledge, maybe helped plan the heist, or you just got incredibly lucky." It was clear by her tone which scenario she considered most likely.

"Lucky?" He smiled, hoping she would let the subject drop. "Honestly, I swear I had nothing to do with it, but as far as how I knew, I'd rather not say. I don't know if the guy you arrested has friends." Would she understand the implication?

Cocking her head to the side, her gaze roamed over Mark as the corner of her mouth turned up. "I should push you on this, but someone like you wouldn't lie to me, would you?"

"Someone like me?"

She raised an eyebrow. "You look like a freaking boy scout."

He grinned. "I actually *was* a Boy scout. Didn't quite make it to Eagle, but the camping trips were a blast." The grin melted away. "I swear to God I had nothing to do with the robbery."

She took another sip of her drink and he tried not to focus on her mouth as she did so. "So what was it? A premonition?"

Could he reveal that much? Did people believe in premonitions? He shrugged. "Something like that." Mark pulled his attention from her mouth and used a napkin and scratched a bit of dried up ketchup off the table.

"Do you have them often?"

"Lately, yeah."

"Did you have one about this meeting? About me?"

His head shot up. Was she flirting with him? "Uh…"

"It's true I had questions about your source of information, but I never considered you a suspect." She lifted one shoulder. "I figured the perp was lying. I actually just wanted to thank you." Her cheeks had taken on a pink hue. "The guy we brought in had several outstanding warrants for some violent crimes. Whether he was intending to rob the gas station is irrelevant now."

"You're welcome." Mark sat back, unsure what else to say.

The detective balled up her cheeseburger wrapper, and set her drink on the tray. "Well, I guess I'll see you around."

"Yeah, I hope so." He realized he did hope he would see her again. He opened his mouth to ask her out, but hesitated. Was she allowed to date someone who had given a tip? It wasn't like there was anything unethical about it that he could see. Not like a doctor-patient relationship.

She shrugged back into her jacket, then stood, tray in hand. Mark rose too, and touched her arm. "Wait. I wondered if…if I could see you again?"

Her eyes met his, a glint of humor showing. "I probably shouldn't agree to it, but sure? Why not? When?"

It wasn't the most enthusiastic response he had ever received, but then again, it was one of the strangest lead ups to a date that he could remember. "Great! How does Friday sound? Can I get your number?"

Detective Bishop dumped her garbage and set the tray on top of others before she reached into her jacket pocket and pulled out a business card. "That's fine. You can call me at the precinct."

He took the card. "Detective Jessica Bishop." It was strange finding out her first name after asking her out. "Jessica. Nice. I'll be in touch."

* * *

"How's your steak?" Mark took another bite of his own. He had ordered medium rare, but it was more like medium well. He hoped Jessie's had turned out better.

"It's...okay." Jessie smiled, but he could see the gray hue of her steak and he was pretty sure she was just being polite.

The beef seemed to form into a ball of lead and settled in his stomach with a thud. This date had not turned out at all like he had hoped. First, Jessie had called saying she was running late and asked if she could meet him at the restaurant. Mark almost asked for a rain check, but worried she would think he didn't have much interest in dating her, when in truth, he was just worried about cutting it too close. At least if they drove their own cars, he could hit the mini-mart afterward without her there to witness the event.

He canceled his reservation at the nice steakhouse because restaurant couldn't change the time to accommodate Jessie running late, and he then had to call Jessie back to let her know where to meet him. He was surprised she still agreed to go because it wasn't that great of a restaurant, but his choices were limited due to needing to find someplace in close proximity to where the shooting would occur.

On top of all that, dinner service was slow. Mark glanced at his watch. Damn, it was already pushing nine p.m. He shoveled in a mouthful of food in an attempt to eat faster but how could he rush Jessie? Was he supposed to skip an offer of dessert? He stole another look at his watch. A couple of minutes after nine. He considered blowing off the save. The kid got what he deserved for trying to rob someone, but guilt didn't just knock on the door to his conscience, it tried to beat the door down. Chagrined at his thoughts, he remembered how young the robber was, and how it had been a fake gun. He was a heartless bastard for even considering letting the kid die just so he could have a better date.

After a few more minutes ticked by and Jessie still had most of her meal to eat, he grew desperate. He had to leave now if he was going to make it on time. As a last resort, he clutched his stomach and grimaced.

"Mark? Are you okay?"

It wasn't hard to fake his distress. "I'm sorry, but I think I'm going to have to cut this short. I'm…I'm on some antibiotics, and sometimes they tear up my stomach." He wanted to choke on the lie, especially when her expression became concerned. She waved for the waiter and Mark asked for the check.

When she reached for her purse and pulled out a credit card, Mark eased up on his act enough to wave her off. "Oh no. I have it."

She walked him to his car, instead of the other way around and with him being 'sick', he couldn't suggest going out for a drink or anything.

They stood awkwardly, and finally she gave him a peck on the cheek. "Call me tomorrow. I want to know you're okay."

Anger at the stupid kid who practically asked to be killed simmered in him, ready to boil over. He glanced at the clock. He didn't have time to waste being angry. The shooting would take place in only ten minutes.

* * *

Mark didn't know what to get, but he needed to purchase something, or at least look like it and do it soon, so he could be next behind the teen. He grabbed a carton of ice cream from a chest freezer near the door and got in line behind the teen. There was no gun visible. He decided to wait until the gun came out and then just make a grab for it. There was no danger since it was a fake, and he had five inches and probably thirty pounds on the teen.

The door to the store opened, and Mark heard a gasp. He shot a glance towards the sound. *Jessie?*

"Mark?" She sent a pointed look towards the ice cream in his hand. At first, he didn't understand her glare. Then he realized that a man with a stomachache probably wouldn't be out buying ice cream five minutes later.

"I can explain." In the few seconds it took him to utter the sentence, the teen moved up to the counter and yanked the gun from within his baggy sweatshirt.

Distracted, and not ready for it to happen so quickly, he didn't process that the robbery was in progress already.

"Freeze!"

Mark turned to Jessie, his jaw dropping in shock at the gun pointed at the teen. *Jessie? She* was the shooter? She couldn't know it was a fake gun at that distance.

He leaped between the teen and Jessie. "No! Don't fire! It's a fake gun! Don't shoot, Jessie!"

"What the hell are you doing, Mark? Get outta the way!"

Mark held his hands up, palms out as he said in as calm a voice as he could muster, "Listen, it's a fake gun. Just a water pistol or something."

Her glared scorched past him and landed on the boy. "Is that true?"

Mark risked a glance over his shoulder. The teen nodded towards Jessie and dropped the gun. The unmistakable sound of plastic hitting the floor made Mark's knees go weak with relief.

Jessie's posture relaxed, and her shoulders rose before they wilted and she let out a deep breath. "Dammit, Taylor. I should just shoot you and be done with it."

CHAPTER FOUR, July 2001

As the novelty wore off, the camera became part of his everyday life. Mark sat at his desk and stared at his accounting records. He was losing money. Had he really canceled that many jobs? It hadn't seemed like a lot at the time, but they added up. What was he supposed to do? He couldn't control when someone needed to be saved.

On top of that, Chicago P.D. had called him in for questioning in several cases. Some incidents stemmed from when he had given them tips and they became suspicious, and other times simply because he had to call in police or the fire department to help him save someone. After one fire in which he saved a family by waking them when their smoke detectors didn't sound, the fire chief had practically accused Mark of arson.

The cherry on top of the pile was staring back at him from his spreadsheet.

"Damn it!" He shoved the computer mouse across the desk. Giving up the camera was out of the question, but he couldn't go on like this either. He'd be homeless before long.

Homelessness held no appeal to him, so he created a schedule and stuck to it as much as possible. While he couldn't control the times of the incidents he needed to prevent, with careful planning, he could minimize the disruption they caused. Most of the time, he could work around his shoots, but occasionally he had to call the client and ask to start a little sooner or later. Most were fine with it, and some confessed to running late themselves, or wishing it was sooner because they had somewhere to go afterward. He found most people didn't care what the excuse was. They were either going to be okay with it or they weren't. The vast majority of his clients didn't have a problem unless he had to be seriously late, but Mark did his best to avoid that at all costs. To make up for it, when he was with a client he gave them his full attention, pushing the camera and any save he had to do from his mind. It was the only way he could do both successfully.

Every morning, he took a few photographs, but then set the camera aside to work with a client or attempt a save. After taking care of his office work, he had to develop the photos, study them, and go to bed to begin the cycle all over again. There was hardly a moment to eat, let alone go anywhere besides the places the camera sent him on its missions.

His nights out with his friends dwindled to once a month. No matter how hard he tried, he just didn't have enough hours in the day. He wanted to have time with friends and he especially missed dating, not that he had been a Casanova, but he had dated his share of women. He missed their company.

His last date had been the failed fiasco with Jessica Bishop almost a year before. He was starting to feel like a monk.

The excitement of the camera overrode almost all the other desires, but the truth was that it wasn't just his obsession with the camera. It was a matter of timing. Many of his friends were settling down and just weren't available to hang out with him anyway. Others had drifted away, which was the case with Mo. Although he had finally chosen photos for the book and had sent it to some editor, it had been months since he had called Mark with an update. Whenever Mark would call him, he only got voicemail. He figured Mo was avoiding him due to the book. Maybe it hadn't turned out the way Mo had envisioned, but Mark didn't dwell on it. He had too many other things to worry about.

He almost spilled the beans to his parents the first Christmas, but when his dad had introduced him to one of his colleagues from the hospital, the other doctor had politely asked Mark what he did for a living. As he replied, Mark had happened to glance at his father and stopped short at the expression his father wore. He might as well have had a blinking neon thought bubble over his head that said, "My son is an embarrassment."

Flushing from anger, Mark had mumbled something about photography and left the party. He passed a drug store that promised one-hour photo developing. In spite of his usual rule against it, he dropped off that day's film, intending to show his father what he really did, but when the photos came back, the camera had chosen to give him only actual photos that day. Not that it mattered, as his father was called into the hospital for an emergency the next day and Mark wouldn't have been able to have his dad watch him make a save anyway. He took it as a sign that he was meant to keep it a secret.

* * *

Just one more roll of film and he could call it a day. Mark took a deep breath and reined in his impatience. It would be foolish to rush the photo shoot, especially since it was for one of the biggest clients he'd ever landed. It wasn't every day that he had an opportunity to shoot a major print ad that would appear in over a dozen magazines and a few billboards. This one job would pay the rent for the month and then some. It was just that his other camera beckoned—the special one.

He smiled at the kids sitting on the couch, hoping to mask his eagerness to be done. Mark was sure they were just as eager to be done, but they had been real troupers. The stylist had fussed over their clothes and made each child change outfits three times. Through it all, the child models had remained good-natured. He quickly snapped the cover closed and advanced the film to the first frame.

"Okay, guys, this time, I want 'Mom' on the sofa with your daughter cuddled at your side. Jake, you can kneel at the coffee table and eat popcorn," Mark said to the young boy playing the son in this ad. Glancing over his shoulder to the other model, Mark circled his hand around the small fake living room he'd set up in the studio. "And 'Dad' you sit on the other end of the sofa, with your feet up on the table."

The man, in his early thirties, probably close to Mark's own age, eased onto the couch and leaned forward, plucking the remote control off the table beside the bowl of popcorn. He held it up, his eyebrows raised. "May I hold the clicker?"

Mark grinned. "Of course."

The mother made a face and then laughed. "I feel completely at home now."

"What about me? Can I eat the popcorn?"

Laughing, Mark grabbed a handful himself. "Absolutely. This is supposed to look like a real family watching television together. Just don't get any grease on the couch. It has to go back to the store when we're done here." He tossed the popcorn in his mouth, crunching on the salty kernels as he did a few test shots with his Polaroid. Satisfied, he strode over to the stereo and turned the music back on. An upbeat tune started blasting, and the kids lit up and it was just that energy Mark was hoping to capture. The 'parents' settled in, looking for all the world as though they were watching a great movie on the television. The perfect family shot. Mark moved around, snapping from different angles, catching the mother toying with the little girl's hair while the dad nudged the son with his toe, both grinning. The client was going to love this. The furniture, the highlight of the shot, was shown as comfortable, sleek and kid friendly all at the same time.

In a few minutes, he was done and he shut off the music, much to the boy's disappointment.

"We're done. You guys were all fantastic. Go on and get changed and I'll let the client rep know we're finished and you can all get your slips signed."

Mark unloaded the roll from the camera and put it with the other two he had taken of the shoot, and slipped all three into a bag with the date and the client's name on it. He set it on his desk to send in with the rolls from his morning shoot for a different client. These shoots paid well, but he was glad that tomorrow he didn't have any shoots scheduled. Things had been going so well lately, he found he needed at least one day a week to organize sending proofs back to customers and clients, booking shoots, and arranging for delivery of whatever props he needed.

"Bye, Mark!" Jake waved as his real mom tried to hustle him out of the studio. Likely, she was trying to beat the evening rush hour.

"Great job, Jake!" Mark gave him a thumbs-up. He'd have to remember to tell the kid's agent how easy he was to work with.

Over the next few minutes, the rest of the models left and Mark locked up the studio, taking his special camera with him. The second his hand closed over it, the familiar tingle of energy thrummed through his body. He couldn't quite explain it. It wasn't like a shock, exactly, but more of an adrenaline rush or a surge of concentrated energy. He just hoped the camera would produce a future photo today. The two previous days had been a bust. Empty days had occurred a few times before, but thankfully, the magic had always returned. Each time, he had feared whatever mystery triggered the future photos and dreams had dissipated.

Mark strode down the street, basking in the warmth of an early July afternoon. The heat wave of the past week had eased and an occasional refreshing breeze off the lake made it a perfect day. The hot smell of asphalt, exhaust, and the faint scent of chocolate from the Blommer Chocolate factory, wafted through the air.

He stopped on a corner as he waited for the pedestrian crossing light to change and tried to decide what to photograph. So far, it hadn't seemed to make a difference what his subject matter was; if a future photo was going to appear, it would supplant the original subject. Since most of the photos on a roll of film didn't become future photos, just a select few, he had taken to making sure to not waste any shot just to be in a hurry to get the precognitive pictures. He had even been able to sell a few at a small art gallery. He found that using the camera had sharpened his photography skills. Because any picture could turn out to be a future photo, he paid closer attention to the details of what he was photographing so if that picture did end up changing to a future one, he could try to puzzle out if there had been something in the original subject matter that tied it to the future photo. So far, it was still a complete puzzle to him.

The light changed and he crossed as part of a crowd of office workers just sprung from the high-rise buildings that created a canyon in the heart of the city. He was tempted to try to capture the light and shadows, but changed his mind. The buildings were beautiful, with gorgeous architecture, but he had plenty of similar photos. Cabrini-Green housing projects were only a few blocks away. Mark contemplated heading in that direction. About half the buildings had been demolished in the last few years, and mixed income housing had taken their place. He wanted some shots of the projects before they were entirely gone. It was a bit risky but after being in Afghanistan and seeing poverty beyond anything he had ever encountered before, Cabrini-Green didn't seem quite so poor and dangerous. Even as the thought crossed his mind, he shook it off. It was like comparing oranges to coconuts. He was less likely to be shot in a remote Afghani village compared to the likelihood of getting gunned down in the Chicago projects, but stepping on a land mine while crossing a dusty village road carried about the same odds.

By the time he came to Division Street, he had made up his mind. He could take a few pictures, and if it seemed too dangerous, he could always leave. Probably.

He scouted the site for the best angle, and decided that a shot of the sun glinting off the fence that gave the building the appearance of a high rise dog kennel would capture the mood of the place. Like a dog locked in a kennel, the people of Cabrini were locked into a life with little hope of leaving. It wasn't so different from the women of Afghanistan.

He raised the camera to his eye and framed a shot. Would it produce a future photo this time? What if today was the day the camera just stopped working altogether? If it stopped working, he wasn't certain he could go back to his boring and mundane old life. Life had never seemed boring at the time, but looking back, there were only so many parties and bars a guy could go to before they all started blurring together. He snapped off a couple of shots and moved around to the other side of the building. The John Hancock Building made an ironic backdrop. Located at one end of the Magnificent Mile, it looked so close, yet to the residents of this building, it must have seemed about as close as the moon.

What had he accomplished in his life prior to having the camera? Not much. He had a nice photography business, but that was about it. Now he had a purpose and it felt good. It felt right. Saving total strangers wasn't something he ever thought he could do and to think he finally had something in common with his father just blew his mind. He doubted, however, that his dad would see the similarity. His father would see only that Mark hadn't finished college, never mind going on to med school. In his mind, saving people took a medical degree, and that was that.

At times, the responsibility of saving a person terrified Mark. What would happen if he didn't change a picture?

Would hell open up and swallow him? The prospect worried him, but then he would change a picture and someone who didn't even know that they would have died, would carry on with their life, completely unaware of how close they had come to death, and Mark would get a heady rush of satisfaction. How could he give that up?

He snapped away, getting a few more shots of the mesh on this side, but moved in closer and laid on the ground to get a picture of a large blackbird picking at a piece of garbage. The building was just a blur in the background.

"Yo, man. What you doin'?"

Startled, Mark rolled from his belly to his side and squinted up at the boy standing beside him. With a grunt, he rose to his feet and put out his hand. "Hi. I'm Mark. I'm a photographer and just thought I'd get a few pictures of this place before they tear down all the buildings." The kid looked about thirteen. He wasn't quite as tall as Mark, probably about five-eleven, but judging by the size of the hands gripping the basketball he held in front of him, he still had some growing to do.

The kid gave Mark's hand a suspicious glance and ignored it, but he wasn't completely rude as he then warned, "This probably ain't the best place to take pictures."

Mark nodded. "I know. I just wanted a few shots. I figured it would be safe enough during the day."

"This place ain't never safe." The kid cast a wary look around. "This corner belongs to the Gangster Disciples. They know me and know I just wanna go play ball and don't want no trouble. Most of the time they let me by, but if I was you, I'd get out of here as fast as I could. You don't belong here."

Feeling suddenly exposed, Mark noted the group of young men coming towards them. "Thanks for the advice. I think I'll take you up on it."

The kid lifted his chin in acknowledgement. "No problem, man." He jerked his head towards the approaching group. "Tell them you was lost and asked me for directions. I don't want no trouble." With that, the boy hurried the opposite way from the group heading towards Mark.

His mouth dry as the dusty grass, Mark decided not to wait for the group to reach him, and instead turned and crossed the street mid-block. Raucous laughter chased him, mocking his actions. He didn't care. One guy against a gang would have been stupid. Fortunately for him, the thugs didn't cross the street and give chase.

Feeling he had reached a safe distance away, Mark turned and watched as the group loitered in the area he had just vacated. Not wanting to be spotted, he ducked into the shadows beside a liquor store. Bright red graffiti decorated the side of the building. He wished he had his telephoto lens with him. He watched a series of cars pull up, one of the gangbangers would lean in the window and few minutes later, the car would speed off. Friends? Or drug deals? Mark bet it was the latter and was again thankful to the boy for warning him.

After observing several more cars repeat the stop and go procedure, Mark turned for home, his earlier eagerness to learn if he would get future photos pushing his curiosity about the dealings on the corner to the back of his mind.

* * *

Mark swished the chemicals around, mentally urging the prints to develop faster. He carefully lifted them from their chemical bath and hung them on the lines he had strung over the washtub.

While they dried, he put away all the chemicals and pans and wiped down the counter. The red light had afforded him a glimpse of the pictures, but not enough to tell what was going on. He saw the photos of Cabrini-Green and a sharp pang of disappointment at another day without a future photo stabbed him in the gut. Maybe the magic had vanished. The pang twisted his stomach into a tight knot. There was so much more he could have done.

He left the prints hanging and went out to the studio to pay some bills. It could have been just the disappointment, but his stomach growled so he grabbed the phone and ordered a pizza from a place down the block. After hanging up, he sighed, fatigue stealing over him now that there was no prospect of a future photo. Maybe he had been addicted to the adrenaline rush. Good thing he had never told anyone about the camera. If he had, he would have had to explain why it no longer worked.

An hour later, he tossed a final crust of pizza into the trash and took a last swig of beer. The bottle followed the crust into the garbage. He closed the lid of the pizza box, deciding that the remaining half would make a decent breakfast.

As he stood to go up to his loft, the light above the darkroom caught his eye. He really should take the photos down. Even though there wasn't a future photo, he might have a picture he could sell to a magazine or something. Cabrini-Green had been the subject of quite a few articles about its demolition and there was a chance he could sell one or two photos as a freelancer. He flipped on the regular light in the darkroom, having no need for the red one now, and quickly unclipped the dozen photos he had managed to snap before the boy had interrupted him.

Back in the office, he tossed the prints on top of the pizza box and, holding it like a platter, he carried it upstairs. The box barely fit in his fridge but he was an expert at making room. He shoved the carton of baking soda to the far corner, and slid the box onto the top shelf, snatching the photos and another beer just before the door shut.

Mark plopped onto the sofa and set the beer on the end table before glancing at the photos.

The top one was the photo of the bird, and he had to admit, it was pretty good. He had caught the bird mid-hop and it was looking right into the lens, a remnant of a fast food wrapper clutched in its beak. The housing project rose up in a distinct blur behind it. It was a keeper. His mood lifted a tiny bit as he turned to the next print, hoping it would be as good.

At first glance, it seemed to be one of the photos he had taken, but the group of thugs was already on the corner, and Mark was sure he had stopped snapping pictures well before they appeared. He flipped to the next and spotted a fifth man with the group. Once again, Cabrini-Green rose in the background, but he definitely hadn't taken this photo. He would have remembered taking a photo of the men making a deal.

His breathing quickened. Could it be? He snatched the next photo out of the pile. The fifth man was on the ground along with one of the original group. A car drove off the side of the photo, only the passenger side showed.

A hand extended out of the back window, a gun clutched in the fist.

One more photo showed the scene, and this time, Chicago Police officers were present, but they were obviously too late as the fifth man lay in a pool of blood, eyes wide and sightless. There was no sign of the other person who had been down, so either they had been able to get back to their feet and leave, or they had been removed for some reason. Possibly taken to the hospital, which meant this photo might take place a short time after the other ones.

A woman was reaching into the deceased man's coat, her hand wrapped around something shiny. Mark pulled open his desk drawer and found his eye loupe. He peered at the image through the loupe, recognizing the shiny object as a police badge, and the woman as Jessica Bishop. He set the loupe down with a sigh. Just great.

After looking for more details in the other photos, Mark set the loupe down and sank back. It was only a guess, but it looked like the dead man might have been an undercover cop. Rubbing the back of his neck, he considered the idea that the cop might have been buying for his own use. Or maybe it wasn't a drug deal at all. There were no drugs in sight. The cop might have been having a friendly chat with the group. Mark snorted, not believing his own hypothesis.

Gathering up the photos, he set the one with the bird aside, and put the others in the order he thought they occurred. Excitement and a trace of fear triggered an adrenaline rush, wiping away any traces of fatigue. The possibilities of what exactly happened in the photos made his mind whirl, but It was no use speculating until he had a dream to match the photos.

* * *

The dream played out as it had appeared in the photos with no surprises. The problem was the man gunned down still wasn't positively identified in the dream. Police on the scene speculated that he was undercover from the badge found on him, but they were still tracking down the badge number when Mark woke up. Why hadn't that information been immediately available?

Like the gas station incident, he thought it was too big for him to handle. If he could find the undercover cop first, that would be one thing. He could have tried to warn him, but without a name, he could think of only one person to turn to.

"May I see Detective Bishop?"

He had thought about calling first, but was afraid she might not speak to him. He had tried calling after their date, but had never reached her. He wasn't sure if that was intentional on her part or he had just always just missed her. After about three attempts, he had given up.

The desk sergeant glanced up from his computer. "Is she expecting you?"

"No, but it's really important."

"Yeah, that's what they all say." The man laughed, apparently impressed with his own wittiness. Mark chuckled. Whatever it took to get past the guy.

The sergeant pointed to his right. "Her office is down the hall, first door on the left. Not sure if she's in. If she's not and you want to wait, you'll have to do so out here." He indicated a bench against the wall.

Luck was with him, and Jessica was at her desk. Another desk took up the other half of the tiny office, but it was vacant at the moment. Mark rapped on the doorway.

She glanced up from some file and a cascade of emotions played across her face at the sight of him: surprise, a hint of warmth, and then anger. Her face finally settled into a mask of indifference. "Taylor."

Ouch. Using only his last name didn't seem like a good sign. "Hi, Jessica."

"It's Detective Bishop."

That hurt even more than the use of just his last name. "Sorry. Detective Bishop. I have to speak to you. It's urgent."

"If this is to apologize for our...dinner, you're about a year too late."

"I am sorry about that, and I tried to call to apologize at the time, but that's not why I'm here today."

"What do you need?"

Mark took a step into the office and stood in front of her desk, gripping the back of a wooden chair. "Remember that tip I had on the gas station robbery?"

She sat back, arms crossed, and nodded. It wasn't much, but at least she was hearing him out.

"I have another tip like that, only this time. There's going to be a drive-by shooting over at Cabrini-Green this evening."

"And you know this how? Or do I even want to ask?"

At least he had a better answer this time and he didn't have to deviate too far from the truth. "I was over at Cabrini yesterday shooting photos—"

"Are you out of your ever-loving *mind*?"

"I told you, I was taking pictures. I wanted to get photographs of the buildings. "

"And you could take some, oh I don't know, perhaps over on the Gold Coast or Oak Park. I heard they have some nice buildings. Mansions and," she put a finger to her chin as though thinking hard, "even some designed by Frank Lloyd Wright."

He rolled his eyes. "Yeah, I understand, but they aren't being torn down in the near future, are they?" He had her there and she grudgingly shrugged. "Anyway, why I was there isn't important, but while I was, I heard some guys making plans for the drive-by. Their target is a guy who's actually an undercover police officer."

She sat forward, her demeanor changing, becoming serious instead of sarcastic. "Are you sure?"

"Absolutely certain."

Waving her hand towards the chair, she said, "Have a seat. Now, what's the cop's name?"

"I don't know. I figured you guys would have that information."

"No, undercover operations are kept very quiet—for the cop's protection." She opened her desk drawer and dug around for something, pulling out a legal pad and a pen. "Can you give me descriptions of the shooters?"

Crap. "No. I only heard them; I didn't see them, they...they were in a car. I was on the other side of some bushes and they were parked on the curb. I heard them talking about it."

Her expression hardened and he knew he had lost her again.

She tossed the pen down. "Are you serious? You come in here with news of a shooting, of a cop no less, but have no description of the shooters. All you have to go on is an overheard conversation from some guys in parked car? That's not exactly hard evidence."

"I realize that. I have a description of the car though, and the guy who gets shot."

Sighing, she picked up the pen again. "Fine. Give me what you have."

He saw the car in his mind's eye. "It's a late '90s model Ford sedan. Dark colored."

"I don't suppose you have a license plate?"

Mark shook his head. "Sorry."

Jessica gave him a long look before sighing. "Listen, Mark. What's your agenda?"

"Agenda?" Totally confused, he could only stare at her.

"This just doesn't add up. For one thing, you stick out like…well, you wouldn't go unnoticed at Cabrini-Green, so I'm a bit skeptical that you would get anywhere near a parked car where people are discussing a drive-by. I have a feeling you're trying to, I don't know, impress me maybe?"

Mark's face heated up but whether with embarrassment or anger, he wasn't sure. "Listen, Jessica, you can doubt me all you want, and be pissed because I screwed up our date, but you remember I was right about the gas station, and I'm right about this. If you don't warn this cop, he's going to be murdered sometime around six p.m. How could it hurt to take a few precautions, maybe get in touch with the undercover guy and warn him?"

"I'm sorry, but I don't have time for games."

Calm down. He told himself that becoming angry wouldn't save the undercover cop. He blew out a breath and pushed his hands thorough his hair in frustration. "It's not a game and I don't have an agenda except to prevent the death of a police officer. I gave you accurate information before, and I'm doing the same now." He remembered a detail, leaned forward and said, "The officer is African-American, young, good-looking, and has a scar on his left forearm. It appears to be a healed burn or something."

"I don't know anyone like that in our precinct. Besides, even if I were to believe you, I wouldn't be able to track the officer down by your vague description. In fact, your alleged victim probably isn't from a precinct near Cabrini-Green. They wouldn't chance him being recognized as a cop, so they'd bring in someone who has never patrolled in that area."

He couldn't leave without a promise that she would do something to prevent the shooting. "But you could ask around. Even if he isn't from your precinct, I know that you'll be involved."

Standing, she put her jacket on and shot him a sharp look as she adjusted the cuffs. "And just how do you know that?"

Mark's mind went blank as he tried to form a reply.

With a knowing look, she nodded. "I thought as much. Here's what I think you're doing. You were right before. You got lucky and overheard a conversation about the gas station robbery. You liked that feeling of power and you're seeking it out again."

"You're wrong." Mark stood. "And I am sorry about our date. Especially now, since you're too angry to listen to me. I hope someday you'll believe me." He turned and left.

* * *

Mark parked a few blocks from Cabrini-Green, his camera sitting on the passenger seat. It was his excuse for being there, but that was the extent of his plan. He drummed the steering wheel. He could leave right now and go back home. It wasn't like he hadn't tried his best to prevent the shooting. It wasn't his fault that the police didn't believe him. He had done his best and that was all there was to it. Yep. It wasn't his problem. Mark turned the key in the ignition, but sat in the idling car unable to drive away.

He slammed his hand against the wheel. *Damn it!* Why did guilt keep beating at the door to his conscience? What did he know of drug deals and drive-by shootings? Only what he saw on the news or on TV shows. The shadows on the street lengthened and he sensed time running out. If he hesitated long enough, he wouldn't have to make a decision. Even if he went to the scene, he didn't have to do anything. That was it. He would just go there and if he happened to see a chance to warn the undercover cop, he'd take it, but that was it. He didn't have to go barging into the drug deal.

With a savage twist of the key, he pulled it from the ignition and grabbed his camera off the seat. Five minutes later, he stood across the street from the projects. He removed the lens cap from the camera and pretended to take a few shots, but used the long lens to get a better view of the area. It only took him a few seconds to identify the corner depicted in the photos and dream. It was close to where he had taken photographs the day before. He lowered the camera and crossed the road. At the moment, the corner was empty, but a few guys were heading towards it from the other direction. He tried to see if one of them was the victim but Mark was too far away to see either man clearly, and he didn't want to be obvious about it by looking through the lens right at them.

The men reached the corner ahead of him, and a car skidded to a stop right at the corner. Mark flinched, certain it was the shooter, but the make of the car was wrong. A man exited the vehicle and sauntered to the corner. Mark caught a glimpse of a scar on the man's arm.

He picked up his pace, almost jogging to get to the cop before the man reached the corner. This was his only chance. "Hey!"

The guy glanced over his shoulder, flashing a look of annoyance at Mark. "Get outta here, man." He didn't even pause, just shook his head and continued to the corner.

A squeal of wheels sounded behind Mark and without looking, he knew this was the car. The dream played in his mind and even with his back to the vehicle, he could 'see' it fishtail around the corner. Any second, it would reach them and bullets would fly. Mark put on a burst of speed and shouted, "Get down!"

The undercover cop turned back a split second before Mark barreled into him. The camera around Mark's neck dug into his chest, the strap tightened and released as the camera hit the pavement. Fleetingly, he registered that it was a goner and he was glad it wasn't the magic one. Shots sounded, men cursed and tires screeched. Mark's flying tackle sent them both to the ground. A deep, bruising pain centered in his left thigh an instant before his right knee exploded with a hot flash of pain as his kneecap smashed against the pavement. Eyes clenched, he added his own foul language to the chaos as he tried to keep from puking. So intense was the pain in his knee, he almost forgot about the other pain in his thigh.

The car sped past, more bullets spraying the air, some hitting the pavement. Mark ignored the pain in his knee and the growing ache in his leg, and huddled with his arms over his head. The cop held the same position, but as soon as the car was down the street, the cop jumped up, his weapon in his hand and ran for the cover of his car. Mark rolled onto his back, grateful the cop was still alive and the pain in his knee was easing. He must have just hit it in the right place. Gingerly, he bent his leg, flexing it a few times.

He sat, becoming aware of a burning in his elbow, and turned it to examine the scrape, but a sudden wave of dizziness assaulted him and his stomach did a flip as he stared down at his blood-soaked thigh. Confused, he wondered if his elbow had dripped, but the slight scrape on that joint was oozing only a trickle of blood.

A car door slammed and a radio squawked. Quick footsteps sounded on the sidewalk. Mark tore his gaze from the wound in his leg to see who was approaching, and a shiver shook him, increasing to a hard trembling that he couldn't control.

The undercover cop crouched beside Mark, one hand gripping his gun, the other a radio. He glanced over his shoulder and made a quick survey beyond Mark before he fixed his focus on him. "Who are you and what the hell are you doing here? Now I gotta call this in and my cover will be blown! Do you have any idea what you just did?"

A reply formed in Mark's mind, but he lost it before it reached his mouth. He blinked as the edges of his vision darkened.

The officer fixed him with a glare, but then his eyes flicked down and widened. "Shit! You been shot! Lay down." He pressed a hand against Mark's shoulder, helping him lie back on the sidewalk.

"Yeah. Okay." The pain that had been muted in comparison to his knee now screamed through his leg as though it had been waiting its turn to make itself known.

Mark licked his lips, suddenly thirsty. The dizziness persisted despite lying down, and the sight of the white puffy clouds floating overhead made his stomach lurch. He closed his eyes and draped his arm over them to try to block out the nausea along with the sky.

Distantly, he registered the cop calling out on his radio and undecipherable chatter as the officer rattled off a bunch of numbers and asked for a bus. That confused him, but for some reason, he thought he should know what it meant. He forgot all about it when the cop leaned on Mark's wound. With a strangled groan, Mark reflexively grabbed at the man's hand to remove it.

"Sorry, man. I have to hold pressure here before you bleed out on me."

Mark wasn't sure if he lost consciousness but one second it was just him and the cop and the next, there were sirens and a multitude of voices. Mark struggled to keep his eyes open to see what was going on but the sirens and voices faded.

* * *

Absently twirling a pen through her fingers, Jessica puzzled through Mark's story. It still baffled her. She hadn't been aware of any officers operating undercover in the Cabrini-Green projects, but that didn't surprise her. Undercover operations were always kept under strict secrecy. It was for the protection of the undercover officer.

It only took one person with a careless remark to blow the cover. She wasn't even sure who to ask. It wasn't like she could repeat Taylor's description because if by some chance, he actually had overheard that conversation, and there was someone who met that description, she could be putting the cop in danger instead of helping him. In the likelihood that Taylor hadn't heard a thing, but was making up this story for some crazy reason, just by snooping around she could jeopardize the officer and the operation.

Tapping the edge of the pen on the folder, she shook her head. The scar on the cop might not even be real if he was undercover. The pen froze. How had Taylor obtained a description of the cop? He hadn't seen the officer, just supposedly overheard a threat against him. She doubted very much that thugs planning a hit would describe their target as young and good looking. That shed doubt on his story. The idiot.

She hated to waste even more time dealing with Taylor's story, but she thought she would pay him an official visit later, maybe threaten to arrest him for filing a false report. That would teach him to get his thrills somewhere else. Jessica pushed the papers back into the folder and sorted through various post-it notes looking for the one she had used this morning to jot down Taylor's information. She found it, but she hadn't taken his phone number. *Stupid.* Well, he was a commercial photographer, it shouldn't be too hard to find. She pulled out a phone book and flipped to the yellow pages.

Her partner Dan poked his head into their shared office. "Hey, we just got a call. Guess we didn't make it out of here on time."

Jessica glanced at the clock. Thirty more minutes and the next shift would have been the lucky ones covering the call. "What do we have?" She removed her jacket from the back of her chair and slipped it on as she followed him out to the unmarked car.

"A shooting at Cabrini."

The hair on the back of her neck stood on end and she came to a dead halt. "Are you serious?" Maybe Taylor had called Dan too, and now her partner was pulling her leg.

He glanced over his shoulder with a puzzled expression. "Of course I'm serious. Come on— shake a leg. Time's wasting."

She shook her head. It's not like a shooting at the housing project was unusual. Any idiot could claim there would be one on any given day and the odds would be good they would be correct.

Lights on and siren blasting, they approached an intersection. She checked her side for traffic and called out, "All clear."

It took them six minutes to reach the scene. A marked squad had beaten them, and they parked behind it. An officer was busy keeping onlookers from pushing too close. Jessica scanned the crowd, wondering if any of them had witnessed the shooting. They all would need to be questioned, but she turned her attention to the activity on the sidewalk where a man appeared to be aiding another who lay sprawled on the pavement. Blood pooled on the sidewalk and flowed like a river to the edge, darkening the dead yellow grass to a deep magenta.

"Damn." She quickened her steps. "What happened, and where's the ambulance?" She wondered why the officer controlling the crowd hadn't taken charge of the scene. He should have been the one at the victim's side until trained help arrived.

The man rendering aid glanced up, but kept a hand tight against the injured man's thigh. "I called it in, but this isn't exactly their favorite place to respond to a call."

"Who are you?"

When the man shifted to look at her, she caught a glimpse of the victim and froze. *Mark Taylor?* Even with his eyes closed and his skin ashen, she was sure of it. What the hell had he gotten himself into?

Dan, following close behind, bumped into her after her sudden halt. His hands gripped her shoulders to keep her from jolting forward. "What's the problem, Jess?"

She took the final few steps to reach Taylor's side. "I know this guy."

Dan glanced at her in concern as he stepped up beside her. "Is he a friend or something? Should I call in a replacement for you?"

With a shake of her head, she said, "No, I'm okay. I dated him once. He came to me with a tip about—" She stopped and closed her eyes for a moment, unwilling to admit that she had been given a tip she hadn't acted upon. "*Shit.*"

"What?"

She made a sharp gesture towards Mark. "This! *This* is what he tipped me about, but he had no proof, no sources... nothing I could go on." She knew she spoke the truth but guilt still slipped under her professional armor and poked at her conscience. Her anger at Mark for ditching her on their date last year shouldn't cost him his life. If she was honest, it wasn't just the bad date, it was the fact that she would have shot that boy with the fake gun if he hadn't stopped her. Her ego and pride, in addition to denying her own infallibility, might cost Mark Taylor his life.

Dan's eyes narrowed as his brow furrowed in puzzlement. "He tipped you that he was going to be shot at Cabrini-Green?

Shaking her head, she took a deep breath. "No, not that he would be shot, but that someone would be shot." Now wasn't the time to go into details with so many people around. She still had to sort it out in her own mind. Mark had never mentioned that he would be here. If he had, she would have warned him away. *Damn him!*

"Interesting. Well, let's see what the story is."

Jessica nodded. It was better not to jump to conclusions. The likely story was that Taylor somehow instigated the shooting to gain credibility. It wouldn't be the first time someone tried to organize a stunt to get attention and then had it totally backfire. She crouched beside the man assisting Taylor. "Did you witness what happened?"

"Witness? Hell, no. I didn't see a damn thing. This guy planted me face down on the pavement."

"Was he the shooter?" A part of her prayed the answer would be no. Taylor hadn't stuck her as that desperate for attention and if he had done this, then her cop instincts were about as accurate as a report from a drunk witness.

"No. The shots were fired from a blue Thunderbird. Probably a mid-'90s model."

Jessica took a long look at the man. His phrasing was more like a cop than a gangbanger. "Are you a police officer?"

He turned and swept his gaze over the crowd, before nodding. "Yeah, but keep your voice down." He gave a warning nod to the gathering onlookers.

His eyes widened in surprise before they narrowed and his mouth set in a hard line while he swept a glance around. Quietly, he replied, "I was, but it's blown now. Wade Phillips out of 12."

Dan pulled gloves from his pocket and snapped them on. "I'll hold pressure."

Phillips nodded. "I think the bullet hit an artery or something. He's bleeding like a son of a bitch." They made the switch, and Taylor groaned when Dan took over. Jessica saw his eyelids flutter and his right arm moved as if to push at Dan's hand, but it flopped back down before reaching its goal. She swallowed hard and focused on Phillips. She had to find out what happened now, while his memory was still fresh.

Still kneeling, Phillips let out a sigh as he sank back, his forearms resting on his thighs, his bloody hands held awkwardly as though to keep them from staining his clothing. She hated to break it to him, but his baggy shorts had already soaked up a good portion of Taylor's blood. Sirens sounded and she turned, relieved to see the ambulance finally make an appearance.

"Come on, Phillips. I have some wipes in the car. I need to ask you a few questions, too." She welcomed the chance to do something useful.

He followed her to the car and she waited while he used the wipes, almost cleaning out their supply as he scrubbed his hands. A plastic grocery bag, tangled in a weed on the parkway, flapped in the breeze. Jessica ripped if from the weed and held it open for Phillips to toss in the used wipes.

Knotting the bag, Jessica tossed it onto the front seat of the car and pulled out her notebook. She wondered if she appeared as shaken as she felt. "So, what happened here?"

Phillips shrugged. "I have no idea. I've been working on this case for two months, and now it's blown. Two months' work is gone. I might as well have wiped my ass with it and tossed it down the toilet." His lip curled as disgust and anger warred for the dominant expression. "I've been living like a goddamn gangbanger so I can catch this scum, and now my cover is blown because I had to call in this shooting or let this guy die."

Jessica could sympathize. She had done a few undercover assignments before and knew how hard it was to play a role for weeks on end. For it all to then get wiped out was one of the most frustrating feelings in the world. "I'm sorry about that, but you did the right thing."

"Who the hell is he and what was he doing on my corner?"

"I know him and he's not a bad guy...just a bit different. He said that he heard something might go down here this afternoon, except he had no evidence to back up his claim. "

"He tipped you off and nobody took action?"

Jessica stiffened. "Look, I hate to admit it, but I had dated him before and it didn't go well. It was after he had tipped me off to a different incident and I thought he was trying the same ploy to get another date. Besides, he had no evidence and his story sounded more like something a five year-old would cook up to get some attention. I had nothing to go on. What was I supposed to do? Set up a stakeout right here on your corner? Somehow I don't think that would have worked wonders for your undercover operation either."

Phillips glared at her for another ten seconds before he let out a deep sigh. "No. It's cool. I get it." He threw a look over his shoulder at the onlookers and then leaned towards her, his voice lowered. "All I know is that all my work was finally going to pay off. I was about to make a buy on a large amount of cocaine. Not one of the regular street dealers, but someone higher up in the organization." With a shake of his head, he crossed his arms and turned to lean against the car. "Anyway, that's when this guy Taylor came out of nowhere and yelled something I couldn't understand. He tackled me like he was an all-pro linebacker." Phillips rubbed his side and grimaced. "I think his camera hit me in the side, might have broken my rib." He waved a hand towards a camera lying a few feet into the grass near Mark.

"Go get yourself checked out too."

He pushed off the car. "No, I'm okay. So, that was pretty much it. Shots were fired and I got a glimpse of the car, but it took off down the street. I didn't get a plate, but I have a pretty good idea who it was. No proof though."

"Okay. If you think of anything more, you know the drill."

"Right. I gotta go fill out a report. It's going to be pretty sparse on details unless you can find out what this guy's story is." His gaze darted over Jessica's shoulder and grumbled, "And I'd appreciate if you let me know how he is later."

"No problem." Jessica made a move to retrieve the camera and see how Mark was doing, but something nagged at her. She pivoted back to Phillips, zeroing in on his arm and her breath caught. It was all she could do not to snatch his arm for a closer inspection to see if the shiny scar angled across his forearm was real. "Have you ever met Mark Taylor before?"

"No. Not that I can remember. Why?"

She wasn't sure if she should bring it up. By Phillips own admission, he had been working this area for a few months. Taylor could have been observing. He could have seen the scar and added that detail to try to give his story the ring of credibility. "Nothing. Just wondered."

For now, she would keep Taylor's tip to herself until she had a chance to question him further. Dan had stepped aside when the paramedics arrived and was now asking anyone in the crowd if they had witnessed the shooting. Jessica watched as Taylor was loaded into the ambulance and then joined her partner.

* * *

Mark hobbled from the bathroom to the chair in the corner of the hospital room. He leaned the cane the physical therapist had given him against the arm of the chair and sat back with a sigh. Lunch would be coming soon, and if he was lucky, he would only have two more hospital meals to contend with before he was discharged tomorrow. He had never been a patient before and vowed he never would be again. The food sucked, and they didn't let you sleep for more than an hour at a time without coming in to poke you with various objects like a needle or thermometer. He picked at the piece of gauze taped to the inside of his elbow. When he had finally been alert enough to hear the doctor's verdict on his injury, he had been told that he had lost about forty percent of the blood in his body as the bullet had nicked the femoral artery. They had pumped him full of fluids and transfused multiple units of blood, so he couldn't understand why were they so eager to extract more every day.

At a light knock on his door, he looked up from his arm, half-expecting that his thoughts had conjured up a lab tech with a syringe at the ready. Instead, Jessica Bishop stood in the doorway.

"May I come in?"

Surprised, Mark nodded. "Uh, yeah, sure. Come on in, Jes—uh, Detective." He took a peek down to his lap to make sure everything was covered. The hospital gown was a little short and the nurse said she hadn't been able to find any pajama bottoms for him. A drain dangled from the bulky bandage around his thigh and the bulb was partially full of a thin bloody discharge. He tugged the gown down to cover it.

Her cheeks were flushed beneath a golden tan and he realized she was as uncomfortable with his state of undress as he was.

"Sorry. I would have called first, but I didn't want to disturb you." She gave a vague wave over her shoulder to the hallway. "When I got here I checked at the nurse's station and they said you were awake."

"No, it's fine." He tried not to look at the blanket draped across his bed. If only he could reach it and spread it across his lap.

Her olive blouse, made out of some kind of silky looking stuff, was long-sleeved, but she rubbed her hands up and down her arms and gave a shiver. "It's kind of chilly in here. Can I get you a blanket?"

Mark almost laughed out loud even as he felt his cheeks burn. "That would be great. There's one right there, if you don't mind."

She handed it to him and then examined a couple of flower arrangements on his windowsill while he covered himself. Feeling more secure, but also like an eighty-year old invalid, Mark cleared his throat. "So, um, I take it you're not here just to visit me."

Her fingers lingered on the petals of a daisy as she turned to him. "I'm afraid not."

A stab of disappointment caught him by surprise. Of course. She was here officially.

"Do you feel up to answering some questions regarding the shooting?"

Now he felt even more like an invalid. "Up to it? Sure. I'm fine," he lied. His pain meds had just about worn off and he had been up and moving all morning, including his longest session of physical therapy yet, but he straightened, and rolled his shoulders to ease the tension.

"Good. I have to ask how you really knew about the shooting. Had you been spying on the undercover cop?"

So much for his attempt to relax. His muscles tightened. "No. I told you. I was just there taking photos of the projects. You know I'm a photographer and with Cabrini being torn down a bit at a time, I just wanted to get it on film while I still had the chance."

"The cop who was working that operation isn't buying that story and he's angry at your interference." She paused, her gaze sliding away for a split second before landing on him again. A shadow of guilt or regret lingered in them as she said, "He wants charges brought against you. He's convinced that you blew his cover on purpose."

"Blew his cover?" Mark shook his head, incredulous at the accusation. "I wasn't trying to blow his cover. I was trying…I *succeeded* in saving his life."

"So you say. For all he knows, you stopped him from making the deal or identifying the shooter in the car. He doesn't know if he was set-up by the drug dealer he's trying to bring down, or if it was a rival gang trying to get rid of the competition."

Mark rubbed a hand down his face, suddenly weary. "Look, I'm sorry if I screwed up whatever it was he was doing. I went there with the plan of just trying to warn him, but everything happened so fast, I just…just reacted. I still don't understand how I blew his cover, but if I did, that wasn't my intention."

Jessica crossed her arms and leaned against the sill. "Was it one of your premonitions?"

Warily, he nodded. "You could say that."

She blew out a breath, sending a strand of hair that had escaped her ponytail flying up, and he watched mesmerized as it settled back against her cheek before she said, "I believe you. I have no idea why, but I do."

"Really?" His weariness lifted a degree.

She raised her hand, palm facing him in a stop motion. "Don't sound so surprised or relieved. I believe that you just reacted and didn't intend to blow his cover. I questioned some witnesses and a boy remembers you taking pictures the day before, so that part of your story checks out, but I'm just a little suspicious as to your motives for being there in the first place. Without any other proof, I guess I'm just going to have to write up my report with the information you gave me."

Swallowing hard, Mark tried to smile. "Thanks. I appreciate that." He didn't want to push his luck, but he had one problem that had just occurred to him that morning. "Can I ask a favor?"

"Sure. You can ask, but I can't promise I can fulfill it." Her smile softened the statement.

"Well, nobody seems to know where my car is. I had parked my Jeep a few blocks away, and now it's gone."

"Ah...it's probably been towed somewhere." She reached into the pocket of her jacket and withdrew a pen and small notepad. "Here, write the make and license plate number if you know it. I'll check at the impound lots and let you know. I can't promise that they'll drop any charges though."

Mark jotted them down, and held the pad out to her. "Here. And thanks."

She nodded and then pointed with her chin towards his leg. "So, what's the prognosis?"

"Full recovery." He grinned. When he had been in the ER, he had been pretty out of it from shock and whatever meds they had given him, but he remembered the surgeon mentioning a possibility that he could lose the leg. After surgery, he had awakened terrified his leg was gone. He hadn't been able to feel past the bandages and didn't trust the sensation of his toes wiggling. He'd heard of phantom pains in amputated limbs. His leg had been elevated and he hadn't even been able to touch it with his other foot. It wasn't until the next morning when his leg had been uncovered and he was able to sit up a little and see his toes that he had believed the doctor that his leg was still attached.

Jessica smiled. "Glad to hear it."

The grin slipped a little when their eyes met and held. She dipped her head and he swore her cheeks pinked. Did they still have a connection? He felt it, but if she had, she didn't let it show as she pushed off the sill, smoothing her blouse and tucking a little fabric into the waistband. "Well,

I guess I'll let you get some rest. You're looking a little pale."

Her comment about his lack of color killed any fantasy that she had felt anything other than maybe a passing worry that he might pass out any instant. "I'm fine, but I hope I cleared up any questions you had, *Detective*."

"*Detective*? Reverting to formality?"

"It seems appropriate."

She paused as she turned toward the door. "I'm sorry you feel that way, Mark. I'm just trying to do my job."

He nodded.

"If I think of anything more, I'll be in touch." She raised an eyebrow and the corner of her mouth turned up. "Or if you decide you know something you haven't mentioned, feel free to contact me."

It was hard to stay angry when she looked at him like that and he felt a grin tugging at his mouth.

* * *

After Jessica left, Mark took a few bites of his lunch and then rested, not awakening until mid-afternoon when his parents came by to visit. He was glad they had missed the detective's visit. All his parents knew was that he had been caught in a drive-by shooting. The doctors hadn't known all the details, and as far as Mark was aware, the police hadn't said anything to his parents, as his folks had nothing to do with the shooting. He was sure his father would have grilled him in front of Jessica if he had been present.

His mom leaned down and kissed his cheek. "Hey, hon. How are you feeling?"

Finding the bed controls, Mark raised the head until he was sitting almost straight up. "Great." The rest had restored his energy. He gingerly moved to sit on the side of the bed. "I feel like taking a walk. You guys want to come?"

His father nodded, but added, "You two go ahead. I saw your doctor out at the desk and I wanted to ask him a few things."

Mark didn't have a good reason to object, but part of him resented his father grilling the doc about his care. As far as he was concerned, the surgeon had performed a miracle in saving both his life and his leg. "Dad, don't piss off my doctor by questioning everything. You know he did a fantastic job."

His dad's eyes widened as he spread his hand over his chest. "I'm not going to question him. I'm just going to suggest a few things he might want to consider in the future when he's presented a case like yours. You know I interned at Cook County, right? You don't spend time there and not learn about gunshot wounds."

His mother gave his dad one of her looks. Even though she spoke in a calm tone, she was annoyed. "Gene, you have trotted out that tidbit of information at least a dozen times since we've been here. Mark's doctor is a busy man—just like you are when you're making your patient rounds." The annoyance melted and she smiled and brushed her hand across his father's hand, twining her fingers in his. "Come walk with us."

Although he appeared torn, Mark's dad finally nodded. "Fine, but I'm going to speak to him before Mark is discharged." He turned to Mark and asked, "By the way, have they told you when that would be?" Before Mark could reply, his father said, "I should find the doc and ask how Mark's labs are and if his white count is still up. If it isn't, a course of oral antibiotics would be appropriate."

Mark rolled his eyes. "Look, Dad, my doctor is doing a fine job. I'd appreciate it if you stayed out of it." He leaned forward and snagged the cane from where he had propped it against the bedside table. As he positioned it to stand, he caught his dad's stunned expression. He hadn't intended to hurt his dad's feelings. Guilt heated his face. "Sorry, Dad. It's just that I can take care of my own health." In the process of standing, Mark couldn't speak for a moment and stood, catching his breath and waiting for the wave of pain to pass. As he became accustomed to it, he finally let out the breath. He opened his mouth to thank his dad for the concern, but before he could, his dad spoke.

His arms crossed and his face was hard as stone, he said, "Really? So you're on top of everything?"

On top of everything? What the hell was he talking about? Why did he always have to use that tone? The tone that said Mark was an idiot.

"Yeah. I think I am. The doctor said I'm making a remarkable recovery so I don't need you butting in. I can take care of myself."

"I have to wonder about that. You seem to make a lot of bad choices."

"Excuse me? What the hell is that supposed to mean?" He straightened as much as he could.

His dad swept a hand towards the cane. "You chose to take pictures in a gang infested neighborhood. Did you really think that was a good idea?"

Jaw clenched, Mark fought the impulse to give up his secret. His dad wouldn't understand. Prophetic dreams?

Yeah, right. He wasn't going to open himself up to that ridicule. Even with the photos, his dad would scoff in disbelief and probably accuse him of manipulating the photo on his computer. If by some wild chance he believed everything, he'd advise Mark to turn the camera over to the police and then suggest that if he wanted to play at being a superhero, he should have become a doctor—like him.

Tension thickened the air as he locked eyes with his father.

His mom cleared her throat and moved to retrieve a bag off a chair beside the bed. "I almost forgot, Mark. I brought you the clothes you asked for plus I included a pair of sweatpants. They should fit over the bandage."

Mark tore his attention from his dad and attempted to smile to show his appreciation. "Thanks, Mom. That's great. In fact, if you help me get them over my foot, I'd like to wear them now."

CHAPTER FIVE

Mark limped across the loft and fished the phone out of the sofa cushions. The sound of the ringing had been so muffled, he wasn't sure what it was at first.

"Hello?"

He hadn't had time to look at the caller ID before picking up as it had taken him about five rings to answer and voicemail would pick up before the sixth.

"Hello, Mark? This is Jessica Bishop…Detective Bishop."

He smiled at the clarification, as if he knew some other Jessica Bishop. "Hello, Detective. Sorry I never called you back, but I couldn't think of anything new to add to what I had already told you."

"Oh no, that's not what I was calling about. I was just wondering how you were doing."

A warm glow of pleasure sparked in his chest. "I'm doing great. I even ditched the cane a few days ago."

"That's wonderful. Glad to hear it. Do you have to go to physical therapy or anything?"

Mark eased down onto the sofa, bringing his injured leg up, trying to bite back the grunt of discomfort the action caused. "Yeah, I go every other day."

"I see…"

An awkward silence followed and Mark wracked his mind for something to say to fill it. "Hey, I never heard back about that undercover cop. Is he still going to press charges against me?" The worry had nagged at him ever since she had mentioned it when she had been at the hospital.

There was a pause and Mark held his breath, awaiting the worst.

"No...I don't think so. I haven't heard anything since right after you were shot. I think he was just frustrated. I honestly don't think he had a case against you anyway. You didn't break any laws since you were on a public sidewalk, and in spite of what you told me before, we couldn't find any proof that you intentionally blew his cover."

"No, I didn't. I just wanted to save his life."

She cleared her throat. "Yeah, well that opens another can of worms that I don't care to deal with right now. We're going to say you made a lucky guess, okay?"

Mark grinned. He could handle that. "Sounds like a plan."

"Great. Did you get your car back okay?"

"Yeah, thanks for the help on that. It cost me a few hundred, but the Chicago PD waived the parking tickets. I had to pay for the towing and storage though. My parents picked it up for me."

"Great. Are they there helping you?"

"They were, but they went home yesterday. My father had some patients he really needed to see this week."

"Ah, so he's a physician?"

"Yeah."

"Okay, well, um, do you need anything? It must be hard getting around right now."

His mother had stocked his fridge and cupboards, so he didn't need anything, but he wasn't about to pass up an opportunity. "Well, actually, there is one thing I could use."

"Sure. What is it?"

"Toothpaste." Mark closed his eyes and shook his head. It had been the first thing to come to his mind and he had just blurted it out. He had a whole tube of the stuff in the bathroom, but now she was going to think he was sitting here with plaque-coated teeth.

She laughed. "Toothpaste? Any particular brand?"

"No, just something minty." As if ninety-nine percent of them weren't minty. Another brilliant answer. He was on a roll.

"Okay. One tube of minty toothpaste. Got it. I hope this isn't a toothpaste emergency or anything, because I just remembered I have to run by my sister's house tonight, but I'm off tomorrow, so I could come by about mid-morning."

"Tomorrow is fine. I'll...I'll just give the tube I have another squeeze up from the bottom. I'm sure there's enough to get by." He didn't want her to think he was skipping on brushing or anything. He gave her his address and told her to buzz and to give him a little time to get to the buzzer.

After hanging up, he almost did a jig — he would have if he had been able to. Instead, he made do with a fist pump.

* * *

Mark leaned on the refrigerator door searching for something he could offer Jessica when she arrived. Milk. No. Beer. Nope, it was too early and it didn't feel right. Orange juice? Nah. Well, he could offer it as a last resort, but it wasn't something someone sat around sipping. Ah! Pay dirt. A small pitcher of iced tea hid behind the gallon of milk. His mom loved the stuff and must have made it before they left. He wasn't much of an iced tea drinker, but he was glad to have it on hand. He slid open the lunch meat drawer. Turkey and pastrami. He spotted some bagged greens in the bottom drawer. He didn't know why he was wondering about all this. It wasn't like she mentioned staying for lunch. In all likelihood, she would drop off the toothpaste and leave.

When the buzzer sounded a little before eleven, he let her into the building then ran a hand through his hair. Sheesh. It wasn't like he had never spoken to a woman before and he was ready to evict the butterflies in his stomach. At the tentative knock, he made himself pause a few seconds before opening the door so she wouldn't think he had been standing right by it waiting for her.

As soon as he opened the door, she tilted a box of toothpaste towards him. "One tube of minty toothpaste." The corners of her mouth tilted up and her eyes sparkled.

Mark took the tube and swept his hand out. "Thank you. Come on in."

Jessica glanced around after stepping in. "Nice place. I like the wood and brick accents."

"Thanks. It's one of those converted warehouses. My studio is on the first floor, but sometimes I do shoots right up here because of the great lighting." He gestured to the large arched windows. "I just shove the sofa out of the way and I can use the brick as a backdrop." He was rambling and shut his mouth before he made a fool of himself.

"I see." She stood, her weight shifting from one foot to the next.

"Speaking of the sofa, have a seat. Would you like something to drink? Iced tea? Water? Orange juice?"

She started to sit, but then straightened. "Iced tea sounds good, but let me get it myself. You're the injured one. I should be waiting on you."

Mark waved her back. "No, I'm fine. I need to work my leg as much as I can. Besides, I've had enough of people waiting on me. It's not nearly as appealing as it sounds."

She nodded. "Yeah, I guess that can get old fast, but at least let me help." She followed him as he limped into the kitchen. "When I saw your wound, I would not have expected you to be up and around, doing this well this soon. You're tougher than you look."

Heat climbed Mark's cheeks at the backhanded compliment. He decided to play along with the teasing. "So, are you saying I don't look tough?" Turning, he straightened to appear as tall as possible, and did the muscle man flex with his arms, his face a stern mask.

Bursting out in laughter, she shook her head. "That's not what I meant, but now that you mention it, if that's your 'mean' look, you better work on it a bit. I think even a shy five year old wouldn't be afraid of you."

"Aw man, that hurts!" Mark shook his head in mock despair and pulled the iced tea out of the fridge.

"Where are the glasses?" Jessica stood in front of the cabinets, her eyebrow raised.

"The one on your right." He pulled out a tray of ice cubes and set them on the breakfast bar alongside the pitcher.

She took two glasses and brought them over. For her, he would drink iced tea. After he had poured two glasses, he pulled a bar stool out from under the bar and slid a second one out for her. "We can sit here instead of the sofa. Honestly, it's easier for me to sit here." He sat with a sigh.

"Great view!"

He was so used to the sight of Lake Michigan in the distance, he had forgotten how lucky he was to have an east view that wasn't impeded by other buildings. By some stroke of luck, there was a thin corridor of low buildings which stretched between his loft and the lakefront. While he was far enough away that the lake was just a thin blue strip, on a clear day like this, it was beautiful.

"Yeah. I got lucky. This building hardly ever has vacant apartments, but I knew the guy who was leaving. He was a photographer too, but decided to pack up and move to New York to try his hand there. He gave me the tip that this apartment and the studio would both become available. Before that, I had a really dingy studio west of here and a small apartment on the other side of the Kennedy. It was a hassle to go back and forth from the studio to the apartment, so even though it costs a bit more, it was worth it." There he was, rambling again.

"Well, it's really nice."

After that, they fell into an easy conversation. They compared notes about their neighborhoods, she offered a cute story about her little niece, and he told stories about growing up in a small town in Wisconsin and how he had been so naïve when he had first moved to Chicago.

Before he knew it, they were making sandwiches. She chose turkey and cheese, with spinach, on wheat bread, and he picked pastrami, cheese and mustard on rye. He said a silent thank you to his mom for leaving him so well stocked. He normally was lucky to have a loaf of white bread that wasn't moldy, let alone a choice of wheat or rye. When he told her that he had no idea what else he had, and explained about his mom's shopping expedition, Jessie—that's what she said to call her—laughed and did a little detective work in his fridge, finding red grapes and strawberries, which they added to their meal.

Mark mentioned the wonderful food he had eaten in Afghanistan and that seemed to pique Jessie's interest.

"I kept copies of some of my best photos from the trip, but the rest I gave to my friend, Mohommad. The book is his idea. I was just there to help with the photos. If he ever gets it published, I'll get a percent of the royalty, but it's been a few years, and doubt it'll ever hit a bookstore's shelves."

She shuffled through the photos, stopping on some, her face serious and full of concern. "These are...I want to say gorgeous, but that's not quite right." Holding a photo showing one of the burqa-clad beggars, she shook her head and finished her thought, "Unreal. That's what they are. Unreal."

Mark told her about the trip, about the stark beauty of the land, and the friendliness of the people towards visitors, but how it contrasted with the brutality he had witnessed.

It was midafternoon when she glanced at her watch and mentioned having an errand to run before traffic got too bad, Mark felt a pang of disappointment. It had been the most pleasant afternoon he had experienced in a long time, and he didn't want it to end. Asking a woman out on a date wasn't new to him, but this was different because he had screwed up the first date with Jessica and only a brave woman would dare to take another chance after that fiasco. One thing in his favor was that she was a cop, and that meant she was brave. His courage fortified with that rationalization, he limped beside her to the door. He reached into his back pocket for his wallet and pulled out a five-dollar bill.

"Here — for the toothpaste. I appreciate that you took the time to get it for me."

Jessie covered his hand with her hand, not allowing him to remove any bills, and smiled. "That's okay. There's no charge this time." The smile faltered and she shrugged. "Besides, I feel like I sort of owed you one. If I would have listened to your warning, you might not have been shot in the first place."

The last thing he had expected was an apology, and even though she hadn't really said she was sorry, it was pretty close. "You don't owe me anything. I didn't have any proof for you."

She tilted her head. "Why did you go back there if you knew there would be a shooting?"

He almost told her, but decided to use the answer as an enticement to go out with him. "You know, I could tell you all about my motivations over dinner…soon."

"We've been down that road before, Mark."

"I know, and I wouldn't blame you for saying no, but I can promise that nothing like before will happen this time." He felt comfortable making that promise because he was out of commission for a while.

The seriousness left her eyes and she crossed her arms and gave him a flirty grin. "You promise? I suppose we could try one more time. What evening would be a good evening for you to confess your reasons for going back?"

Score! Grinning, he said, "Friday? About seven? Any place in particular you'd like to go?"

She shook her head. "Surprise me."

"Okay. I can do that."

"Can you drive like that?"

He nodded. "Yeah. Good thing it wasn't my right leg." He resisted the strong urge to kiss her goodbye, not wanting to rush her. He would save their first kiss for their date. And this date would be a hundred times better than the first one. Still, it felt awkward standing there, and when she made a move to give him a hug, he leaned into it, wrapping an arm around her. "I'll call you."

* * *

Mark tried to open the car door for Jessie, but his injured leg slowed him down, and by the time he circled the car, she was already out. It was a good thing too, because the valet had barely let her get out before he drove the Jeep down the street.

Jessie raised an eyebrow at the retreating vehicle. "Wow, he was in a hurry."

"I guess I should have driven my Bentley instead of the beater."

She smiled. "A Bentley, huh?"

When he grinned, she caught her breath. The man cleaned up very well, and dressed in a charcoal suit and tie, he could have passed for a movie star. She was glad she had decided to wear her royal blue dress after all. She had almost chosen a more casual dress, but had changed her mind at the last second.

He held his hand out, inviting her to walk a step ahead of him. His hand was warm through her gown as it rested lightly at the small of her back. He did a quick hobble step to reach in front of her to open the door and she almost told him it was okay, that she knew it was hard for him to do these things right now, but she held her tongue, not wanting to embarrass him. She already noted that he was limping less tonight, so maybe his leg was just healing faster than she thought it would.

Besides, she could get used to this kind of treatment. Being a detective and surrounded by a bunch of guys at work, it was inevitable that they began treating her like one of them. On one hand, it was exactly what she had wanted – to be one of the guys— but just because she was a cop didn't mean she didn't want to be treated as a woman when out on a date. She had dated a few police officers, but they had been coarse, like they were on a stakeout instead of a date, and she hadn't repeated the outings with any of them.

"This is beautiful, Mark." She took in the mahogany chairs and matching trim, gold accents and deep red walls. The ceiling was white but had a large oval painted red, giving the illusion that the ceiling was domed. The tables were covered in snowy white linen, keeping the room from appearing too dark, and gilt framed art adorned the walls.

The maître d' showed them to their table, and after he left, Jessie set her small purse on the table and glanced around at the full restaurant. Her mouth watered at the scent of fresh bread and other aromas that wafted from the kitchen. On a cop's salary, she didn't normally eat in a really nice restaurant. "The food must be amazing here."

Mark appeared to be taking it all in too. "I hope so. I've heard good things about it."

"I'm sure it is. I mean, look at all these people. They must know something, right?"

The waiter appeared and asked if they would like a drink to start. Mark raised an eyebrow at her. "Jessie? Do you have a preference?"

"A Chardonnay would be nice."

Mark chose a Scotch. They made small talk while waiting for their drinks and the conversation was a little stilted.

Once the drinks arrived and they had placed their orders, Jessie swirled the wine and took a sip, then set it down. "So…you promised me details."

"Excuse me?"

She tilted her head. "Come on. You said you would tell me why you ended up at Cabrini-Green. I mean, if you knew there was going to be a shooting, why in the world would you go anywhere near there?"

He studied her for a moment, then glanced away and took a long pull of his Scotch. "It's not that big of a deal. I was hoping I was wrong about the shooting, but in case I wasn't, I thought I could help—maybe warn the cop or something."

"So you really were trying to save him? The undercover cop thought you were trying to blow his cover."

He shook his head and studied the golden swirl of liquid in his glass. "No. That would be the last thing I wanted to do."

She believed him. He hadn't even mentioned the lack of thanks he had received from the cop he had saved. "Did you ever consider that you might be shot instead? I mean, it was pretty reckless of you to tackle him. You basically took a bullet meant for him. That kind of makes you a hero."

Mark's jaw clenched, and he set the glass down. "Look, I know I promised you answers, but the truth is, it's not that exciting. I showed up because I was curious. I saw the cop, decided to follow him, and then heard the car come around the corner at a high rate of speed. I figured that was the car with the shooters, and I reacted. That's it. I didn't plan on saving the guy, and if given a second chance, I'm not sure I would do the same thing, so that doesn't exactly make me a hero." After holding her gaze for a moment, he broke eye contact , and rubbed the back of his neck, his expression sheepish. "I apologize. I didn't mean to go off like that. I just would really like to drop the subject and enjoy a nice dinner."

She bit her lip and regarded him. He really believed he wasn't a hero. In her eyes, that made him even more of one, but she just nodded and remarked on how wonderful the hot fresh rolls smelled and took one from the basket.

Dinner progressed, and she was happy that after the tension of discussing the shooting, they were able to fall back into the comfortable conversation style they had shared previously at Mark's loft. The meal was fabulous, and they had decided to split a dessert. They dug in, laughing at how full they were, but it was so good, they couldn't pass it up. She had another glass of wine, but he switched to a soft drink since he was driving.

Afterward, it was still early, and Mark walked her up to her door. She didn't want the date to end, and he didn't seem to either, but as nice as the date had been, she wasn't comfortable inviting him in...yet. The night was gorgeous, with a full moon and about as many stars as were possible to see in the middle of a large city. The air was still soft with only a little chill. On an impulse, she took his hand, and said, "Let's go for a walk."

After an initial look of surprise, he gave her a slow smile. "I'd like that."

"Oh wait. I forgot about your leg."

"It's fine. After such a big meal, and sitting for so long, it'll be good to stretch it out."

He hadn't relinquished her hand, and they descended the few steps from her porch to the ground and strolled down the street. Warm yellow light spilled out of some houses, and laugh tracks to sitcoms floated through open windows, adding to the background noise of distant traffic and an occasional cricket.

Without realizing it, she had huddled close to Mark as they walked. The dress had only thin straps over her shoulders, and goose bumps rose on her skin. Although the day had been warm, the temperature was only low sixties now by her estimate. She should have grabbed a sweater before setting off on the walk.

Mark stopped and looked her for a moment before releasing her hand shrugging out of his suit jacket, draping it over her shoulders. "Here. You must be cold."

She smiled, drinking in the smell of his cologne mixed with his own scent. Pulling it more firmly over her shoulders, she held the edges closed. "Thanks."

Instead of taking her hand, since she was using it to keep the jacket closed, he draped his arm over her shoulders. They continued to walk, and he told her some more about Afghanistan, skipping the brutality he had mentioned before and just focusing on the beauty of the land.

When they circled the block and came back to her house, she slowed her steps, but eventually, they made it to her door. She turned and leaned against it, telling him about how she had never gardened before buying this home, but now she enjoyed planting a few flowers. He listened, and nodded, but stepped closer. Her heart sped up, and her breathing faltered for a moment. He was so close, the familiar cologne now enveloped her, emanating from him and even more enticing. At some point, he had untied his tie and it hung around his neck loosely, the button to his collar undone. She could see the pulse in his neck and it seemed to match her own.

He leaned in, his lips lightly brushing hers, as if testing his welcome. She tilted her head back, allowing him better access, and closed her eyes when the pressure of his lips increased. There was just a hint of rasp on her skin from his whiskers, even though she knew he must have shaved shortly before picking her up because he had that freshly shaved look. The feel of the whiskers didn't bother her at all.

His arm slid beneath the jacket, and rested on her bare shoulder, lightly stroking up and down her arm as the kiss deepened.

She cupped the back of his neck, feathering through the soft hair at his nape, smiling against his mouth when he moaned at her action.

Finally, they broke the kiss. She almost invited him, in, but he stepped back, his breathing ragged. "Can I call you again?"

Call her again? *Hell, yeah!* But she didn't say that. She simply smiled, nodded and slipped his jacket off, handing it to him.

* * *

As Mark strolled along the Michigan Avenue Bridge, he tugged his polo shirt away from his skin to stir a breeze. Summer's humidity had evaporated in the early September air and with winter looming just a few months distant, he wished he could store the heat for future use.

He had one photo shoot scheduled for the day and it wasn't until mid-afternoon. He held the camera, the thrum charging up his arms stronger than he had ever felt before. He rubbed a smudge off the metal body with the edge of his thumb, wondering if the extra energy was because it hadn't delivered a future photo the day before. Did the camera bank energy on days it didn't produce a future photo? It was an interesting idea and he decided he would start tracking the results the day after a quiet day, just out of curiosity.

Aiming at a bas-relief sculpture on the bridge, he took a few photos. Even if it didn't produce a future photo, the shots would be good ones to frame. Maybe he could sell them. Next, he turned towards the river. A few water taxis plied the water and tour boats made their scheduled trips up and down, but no sailboats were heading his way, so there was no danger of the bridge rising any time soon. Monday wasn't the biggest day for boaters anyway. He hadn't really planned to take photos of the river, but he was still basking in the glow from last night's date with Jessie. It had been their one-month anniversary of dating. His mind on the date, he hadn't been paying attention to where he was going. This was as good a place as any other to take future photos. The water sparkled as if strewn with diamonds.

He brought the ram's head on top of the guardhouse into focus, and pushed the shutter. This would be a nice place to propose—when the time was right. Perhaps in the spring. Or Christmas. He grinned. Talk about getting ahead of yourself. What would his parents think of Jessie?

He hadn't even said anything to them yet, just hinted that he was seeing someone. He didn't want to get his mom's hopes up and if he told her too much, she would call him for daily updates.

All he had told them was he was seeing someone and when he was ready, he would tell them the details. He felt a twinge of guilt that he had used his relationship with Jessie to get out of a few trips home this summer. He swept the guilt into the far corner of his mind.

He lowered the camera and slipped his arm through the strap, letting the camera dangle against his side as he leaned against the railing. A breeze carried over the river, ruffling his hair while the sun soaked into his skin. With nothing more pressing than the photo shoot later, the day felt like a holiday. A bike ride would be great. If the shoot went well, he could probably squeeze one in before it became too dark. To get his leg back in shape, he had done a lot of riding, but the last few weeks, he had been so busy catching up on photo jobs he had been forced to reschedule while recuperating, coupled with the future photos he tried to work into his week, he just hadn't had time for a hard bike ride. The only thing that would make the day perfect would be to see Jessie tonight, but she was going to her niece's ballet recital and then out to dinner with her sister and her family afterwards.

Mark pushed away from the rail. His stomach rumbled and with lunch on his mind, he finished out the roll by taking some photos of a large sailboat heading towards him. Done, he ambled off the bridge before it would have to rise to allow the sailboat with its tall mast, through to the locks and out into the lake. His timing was perfect.

* * *

His leg ached after the short, but intense bike ride. Mark did his best to ignore the pain as he pulled on a pair of shorts and a t-shirt after showering. The ache just meant it was getting stronger. Hopefully. He sat on the edge of the bed and rubbed some sports cream into the scar and the muscles around it, wrinkling his nose at the strong scent. He glanced at the bedside clock. Dinner should arrive any moment. Tonight was Chinese and his mouth watered in anticipation. Impatient, he moved to the window and peeked through the blinds to see if the delivery car had parked below. *Shoot.*

Sighing, he pulled his fingers from between the slats and headed to the dark room. Tomorrow he had three bookings. The first one was short, just an acting headshot. He had worked with the guy previously and knew he was easy to work with. Next was a catalog shoot, but it was at a jewelry store, not his studio. Remembering his idea about proposing earlier, he quashed a momentary panic. Just because he was going to be surrounded by diamond rings didn't mean he had to actually buy one. Or even *look* at them. He could just play it by ear. Besides, he probably wouldn't have time to browse. As soon as he finished the shoot, he had to high tail it across town to the John Hancock Center. A client lived on the sixty-fourth floor and wanted good photos of the interior and the gorgeous view overlooking the lake, to help sell the condo. He couldn't even recall what his last shoot involved and supposed he should run down to the studio and check the appointment book, but he was pretty sure it was a look-see to find models for a high end children's clothing line. It made sense because look-sees with kids had to be scheduled after school hours.

Which such a jam-packed schedule, it had crossed his mind to leave the camera on the shelf today. If there were any saves on the agenda, he hoped he would be able to squeeze them in between jobs. If he had to, the Hancock shoot could take place the next day. The client had already said he was flexible as long as it was done before the next week. The only thing he wouldn't have time for would be to get new future photos.

While waiting for the delivery, he prepared the dark room. His buzzer went off just as he finished getting it ready. Perfect timing. He could develop the roll and let the photos dry while he ate.

After paying for the food, he snatched an eggroll out of the bag, eating it as he returned to the darkroom. The roll was hot and crispy. Popping the last bite into his mouth, he swiped his fingers on his shorts and prepared the first steps in processing the film. One day, pressed for time, he had used a one-hour place to develop the film, but the clerk had questioned him about the photos of the bike rider lying in the street covered in blood. The question had caught him by surprise and he had stammered out some flimsy excuse about being a freelance photographer with the newspaper. It wasn't a complete lie as he *had* done some freelance work with newspapers, but the lie about that particular photo didn't fall naturally off his tongue. Afterward, he questioned the wisdom of having his film developed by some place where anyone could inspect them. After that, he avoided any kind of commercial printers for the film from the special camera — no matter how tempting. It could open a complex situation that he wasn't prepared to explain.

The scent of the Chinese food disappeared into the smell of the chemicals as he developed the film. When the first images began to form, he forgot all about eggrolls and fried rice.

What the hell?

How had he managed to get photos of the World Trade Center? He squinted in the red light. No, those had to be some building along the river. He tried to think of any that might resemble the twin towers but came up blank.

As the images darkened, he reached with the tongs, his gut churning as he processed what he was seeing in the photos. He tried to make out details of the photos as they floated in their chemical bath, but the room was too dark. He fought the urge to rush. Whatever these photos showed, it was big. He could see that immediately, but rushing might ruin one of them and it looked like he would need every clue he could get to prevent the unthinkable that seemed to be materializing in his photo tray.

He lost track of time as he stood studying the photos when it occurred to him that it was safe to turn on the lights. Already, he felt a restless energy, a need to do something about these pictures. He snapped the five that showed the horrific images off the line, ignoring the photos of the river and bridge.

He set them on the counter, pushing the bag of food aside as he laid the photos down side-by-side. After two years of acting on the precognitive images produced by the camera, he thought he was immune to any kind of emotional reaction. He had changed too many of the photos for them to even seem real anymore. After all, once he acted, they *weren't* real. They were just images of what might have been. In his mind, they were shadows of the future like in the story *A Christmas Carol*. He shook his head. Not quite like that, but it was a close approximation. But this...this was incomprehensible.

At first glance, Mark had thought that all the images were of the same plane from different angles, but upon closer examination, he could make out the differing logos on the tails and one photo showed a ball of fire. He blinked and took out his loupe, making certain they were different planes. There was no doubt.

His mind whirled with possible ways of averting the disaster, but he couldn't latch on to any one thought long enough to follow it through with a plan of action. Overwhelmed and realizing this was out of out of his league, he picked up the phone, but his finger froze over the number pad. Should he call the cops? Or the fire department? And tell them what? That planes would crash into the World Trade Center? Along with one in a field...somewhere? He wasn't even sure what happened at the Pentagon, but the photo showed a huge fireball in one side of it. Since he had photos of four planes, and three of them were in the process of actually crashing, he guessed that the photo of the American Airlines jet might end up being the cause of the fireball.

His knuckles whitened around the phone. He couldn't even warn anyone tonight. Not without any facts. *Goddamn it!* If he attempted to without any real information it would get him tossed into the psych ward right after they booked him for...well, he wasn't sure what they could charge him with, but he was sure they could find something. Probably filing a false police report, only it wouldn't be false by sometime tomorrow. Why couldn't the photos have time stamps? Or show where the planes were from? Flight numbers would be too much to hope for, but while he was wishing for the impossible, he tossed that wish into the pot with the rest of them.

As he started to process the information, logic took hold. Something like this didn't just occur accidentally. Mark admitted he was no expert, but didn't jets have all kinds of safeguards to prevent pilot errors of that magnitude? His stomach coiled into a tight ball when the implications of what four different planes meant. This was no accident. One plane was an accident, two an unthinkable tragedy, but four? That was somebody's plan.

Setting the phone back on its charger, he drummed his fingers on the countertop as his gaze shot from one image to another, unable to concentrate on just one. How could he stop this? The coil twisted into a knot of pain. What could *he* do? He slammed his fist on the counter, not caring when the blow caused the bag of food to fall over, spilling the contents onto the floor.

With his elbows resting in front of the photos and fingers rubbing circles on his temples, he took a deep breath. *Okay, just settle down and think it through.* It wasn't like this was going to happen tonight. These were all daytime shots, so he had a little time. He raked a hand through his hair as he glanced at the clock. Had it only been an hour since his dinner had been delivered? There was no way he could eat now, but his biggest worry was how in the hell could he sleep? Sleep was imperative so he could dream, but he was so tense and keyed up, it would be elusive tonight.

He circled the breakfast bar and opened the fridge. Four beers. Too bad it wasn't a case, or better yet, a bottle of Scotch, but it would have to do. He opened one and gulped it down while he picked up the cartons of food from the floor. Most of the fried rice had spilled out so he swept it up, but all the while, his mind raced with ideas of how to stop the horror depicted in the photos. He took a long draught of the beer, wiping his arm across his mouth afterward. His goal was to consume enough to relax him so that he could sleep, but a small part of his mind wished he had enough alcohol on hand to erase the photos from his memory. He finished off the beer and chucked the bottle into the trash.

Mark pulled out a second beer and flipped the cap off as he plopped onto the barstool. Why had the camera chosen to show him these photos? Did it really think he could do something about them? He tilted the bottle, already a little buzzed from the effects of drinking the first beer so quickly on a relatively empty stomach. The second eggroll was still warm so he ate it between sips just to put something in his stomach besides alcohol. The goal was to relax, not become wasted.

His common sense struggled to convince him that the camera was just a mechanical device. It didn't think. It didn't *know* that he was helpless to change some things. Maybe this act of violence wasn't really meant for him to change. After all, how could he do it alone? The cold sweat of fear drenched him. If he failed, how many thousands would die? Both towers were billowing smoke in the photos. The Pentagon looked like a side of it had exploded and the other photo, with the plane heading into the field...he shuddered at the terror those passengers would know just before impact. Tomorrow was a Tuesday, so likely all three buildings would be full of employees at work. His hand shook and the bottle rattled as he set it down.

The responsibility for saving all those lives stacked on his shoulders like a thousand bricks. Taking a deep breath, he blew it out and leaning his elbows on the breakfast counter, he massaged the back of his neck. He hadn't asked for this. Since when did purchasing an old camera involve a lifelong commitment to saving the world one photo at a time? There had been no promise—no contract—presented to him forcing him to prevent events depicted in the photos. Sure, he had changed a few things, and had made a difference in quite a few lives, but it was usually just one life at a time.

It wasn't that he didn't *want* to change the outcome of the photos, God only knew, he begged for nothing else, but the magnitude of the tragedy and the multiple focal points made it seem like an impossible task. He had no clue where to start.

He longed to share the burden of knowledge with someone. *Jessie.* As a detective, she would have more experience with something like this, or at least know whom to contact. His fingers closed once more over the phone, but he hesitated. Did he have time to explain the camera tonight and if he did, would she believe him? As a cop, she would want proof and all he had were the photos. If someone had shown him pictures like these two years ago, he would have assumed they were doctored. Jessie would be even more skeptical.

Mark released the phone when he remembered that even if he could convince her of the photos' authenticity, she was out with her sister's family tonight. His time would be better spent looking up numbers of authorities rather than wasted by trying to contact her, and then convince her to come over. It wasn't something he could explain on the phone. Tomorrow he would have more information, and then he could attempt the difficult task of making her believe the photos were authentic and would become reality unless they could stop whoever caused the tragedy.

It was after midnight when he fell into a restless sleep. On his bedside was a pad of paper alongside a sheet of paper with numbers to the FBI, police, ATF, American and United Airlines, some of the major airports across the country and even the White House. He had always been too busy to spend much time on the Internet, but he did some searches and found the non-Chicago numbers listed. He knew the White House was a last resort and he wouldn't ever be connected to anyone important, but he figured it couldn't hurt to have it on hand. The pad was to write down the details as soon when he awoke.

* * *

Mark tossed and turned, trying his best to relax, but it wasn't happening. With a sigh, he flipped onto his back and folded his hands behind his head, staring at the ceiling. How many people were going to sleep for the last time tonight unless he found a way to stop the photos from coming true? He closed his eyes and tried to change the direction of his thoughts. Sleep had to come, it just had to. But instead of sleep, his vision was plagued with images of the planes crashing into the Towers and the Pentagon.

Eventually, his eyes became heavy and he drifted off, only to jerk awake every time as if his mind was fending off the dreaded dreams. After the third time, he sat on the edge of the bed, scrubbing his hands down his face and yawning. Through eyes gritty with fatigue, he noted the time, 2:11 a.m. He groaned. Half the night was gone and he hadn't dreamed at all yet. What if the dreams didn't come? Mark had a sneaking suspicion that he wouldn't be absolved of guilt if he didn't have a dream depicting the events. The photos showed the airlines at least. If he went dreamless the rest of the night, he would have those clues to pass along. The security office at the World Trade Center could be notified, and the same with the Pentagon. At least some people might be saved if he could convince someone to believe him. He padded into the kitchen and drank a glass of water. He prayed that just getting up and moving around would could alter the pattern of suddenly pulling out of the clutches of sleep just as it was getting him in its grasp.

The photos were still on the kitchen counter, and reluctantly, he spread them out for one more look as he sipped the water. Afterward, he went back to bed, and this time when sleep caught him, he didn't escape.

* * *

"Come on...*come on!*" Mark glanced at his watch and paced between the breakfast bar and the sofa. It was seven-thirty already—less than twenty minutes until the first plane would hit. The first planes to crash were probably already in the air or on the runway ready to take off and here he was on hold still on both his landline and his cellphone.

He had been awake for hours already, calling all the numbers on his list, and with the knowledge from the dream, adding a few more, including the New York Fire Department. So far, nobody had taken him seriously. They had asked for his name and number, but then said they were transferring him to someone else. Usually by the third transfer, the call was disconnected. If it wasn't disconnected, he was left on hold so long he finally had to hang up so he could move onto the next number.

The cell was currently on hold for Logan Airport. It was his second attempt with them. The first call had been routed to Lost and Found. He guessed they heard him ask for security and just assumed he was complaining about lost luggage. His intention was to stop the flight from taking off, but as the minutes ticked by, he felt the opportunity to keep the plane safely on the ground slipping away.

On the landline, he waited for the FBI to come back to the line. At least they seemed to listen to his story before telling him to hold for some agent. What the hell was taking everyone so long?

The music stopped playing on the Logan call. *Finally.*

"Yes, I explained to the last guy that you have to stop American Airlines Flight 11 from taking off if it hasn't already. No, this isn't a joke. Listen, there are hijackers on it and they're going to...no, I'm not on the plane, but— wait, please listen...don't put me on hold again. Hello?"

Mark pulled the cellphone away from his ear and looked at the screen, uncertain if they had disconnected him or put him on hold. The screen was still lit and showing the number so he was on hold. There was no music this time.

The FBI line still crackled with various clicks. Did that mean his call was being transferred around to different people?

At 7:35, Logan came back on the line. Someone from the FAA. Mark swallowed hard and answered his question to the best of his ability, "I know you have a situation. I...I dreamed about it. I dreamed about the plane being hijacked. You have to warn the people in the World Tra— Damn it! *Don't* transfer me again!" *Shit!*

The FAA guy had abruptly given the phone to someone else who asked Mark basic questions like his name and address. When they got it all, he was shoved back into on hold hell.

He hadn't even had a chance to warn anyone. Someone finally came on the line for the FBI.

"Please, you have to put me through to someone in charge. There's not much time left. *Oh, God. Please.*"

"I'm sorry sir; I need to ask a few questions first."

"Goddamn it, there's no *time* for questions...time...*oh, shit*...what time is it?" Mark zeroed in on the clock on the VCR. *7:44. No! No! No!* The phone slipped from his fingers as the implication of all those deaths sunk in. It was too late. He had failed. There was no way anyone could stop this now. A voice came from the phone on the floor, and numb with despair, Mark bent to retrieve the phone and put it to his ear. His throat worked, but no words emerged. He tried again, managing to choke out, "Never mind. It's too late."

He clicked the cellphone off. There was no point in trying to warn them again. It crossed his mind to try to stop the other planes from crashing, but it was as though his mind had turned to sludge and the thought took forever to transfer into action. Blinking to clear the fog, he ran a finger down the list of numbers. He had called them all at least once.

Defeat and failure crashed over him and he sank onto the sofa, staring at the muted TV. Any minute now, the rest of the world would know what he had known for a little over twelve hours now. *Good Morning America* was on but the hosts were still blissfully unaware. Charlie Gibson and Diane Sawyer chatted on the sofa before going to a break.

Even if his call to the FBI had gone differently, he doubted that there would have been time. Maybe fighter jets could be scrambled if some were in the area, but even if they were able to intercept the planes, what could they do? Shoot them out of the sky? On Mark's say so? A bitter chuckle slipped out. He shook his head at the absurdity. He didn't even know if there were any bases near New York and it hadn't occurred to him to do an internet search for one. Chalk it up as another strike in the failure column.

A commercial for the *Batman* movie came on and he knew that soon, the news anchors would know. In his dream, every television he saw broadcast the story live as it happened. He didn't know if he could watch it…again, but he made no move to turn the television off. Maybe somehow these photos and his dream were wrong.

The commercial cut off abruptly. He wasn't sure if it was supposed to end that way, but a second later, he forgot all about it as *Good Morning America* returned from the break. Charlie and Diane were still on the sofa, but it was obvious something had happened, for their faces were now serious and seconds later, the screen cut to a live feed of the World Trade Center. Clouds of dark smoke stained a clear blue sky.

Mark's throat tightened and he tried to swallow the sensation of strangling. The constriction descended into his chest, squeezing his lungs. His blood pounded through his body and he felt it throbbing in his neck before it raced through his temples. It pulsed through him as if seeking to escape a fist that clutched his heart.

As the hosts of the talk show tried to sort out what had happened, the second airliner slammed into building two. Even though Mark had known it was coming, he flinched in shock when it happened live on television.

Lacing his fingers behind his neck, he leaned forward, sucking gulps of air. *Shit!* He had failed. Completely and utterly failed.

After the little girl had drowned, he had thought he could never feel worse. He had been wrong.

Mark prayed that somewhere, someone had listened to his warnings and had evacuated the buildings, and it was that thin strand of hope that kept him glued to the news coverage. When Tower Two fell, he grabbed the camera from the coffee table and stood, cocking his arm as he faced the brick wall opposite him. What cruel reason did the camera or whatever controlled the future photos have for showing him something this horrific?

A sob caught in his throat and his arm wavered as his knees buckled under the weight of his grief. What was the purpose of igniting the dreams, if he was helpless to stop what they revealed? The urge to smash the camera against the bricks surged through him, renewing his strength, but the faces of those he had saved in the last few years stilled his hand. How many people in the future would be sentenced to a certain death because he couldn't save them?

With an anguished groan, he lowered the camera. *Damn it!* He couldn't do it. Instead, he strode to his bedroom closet, tossed the device on the top shelf and slammed the door. Turning, he rested against the door, slid down until he was sitting on the floor, and buried his head in his arms.

Mark ignored the phone the first four times it rang, but on the fifth call, he swore and stumbled to his feet, his leg stiff. He picked up his phone too late to answer it, but he went through the missed calls. Three were from Jessie, one from his parents—probably his mom, and one from a number he didn't recognize. Jessie and his mother had left messages on his voicemail but the unknown caller had not.

He moved to the sofa, still clutching the phone, intending to return the calls from Jessie and his mother, but he couldn't. Not now. Maybe later when the pain wasn't so fresh. Mark knew his guilt wasn't rational, that the terrorists were the guilty ones, but he should have been able to stop it. Another wave of anger washed over him, and he turned and whipped the phone against the bricks.

* * *

The camera remained on his closet shelf, the lens glaring at him every morning when he pulled a shirt off a hanger. It sat silent and accusing, a constant reminder of the terrorist attacks—and yet every day it sat unused, was a day that someone might die. Someone he could and should have saved. He couldn't win.

At night, instead of the focused dreams connected to a photo, he was plagued by nightmares filled with ghoulish faces of dead people. Mornings, he awoke in a cold sweat, the echo of terror-filled screams still resonating in his head. There'd been no logic to the nightmares, no way of fixing them.

Remorse finally drove him to pull the camera from the closet. He had seen a story on the news about someone who had died after falling from a back porch. Would that accident have shown up in a photo? It would have been an easy save, but fear that the camera would show him another tragedy he couldn't prevent seized him whenever he thought about using it.

His fear was so great, it took weeks before he could hold the camera, and it was weeks after that before he could actually take photos. If only he could find the courage to develop them. The nights after using the camera, his dreams turned to nightmares and the next day, he avoided watching the news. He was sure that whatever happened in his nightmares would end up being a true story.

It wasn't until November that Mark developed his first film since September 10th. It showed a man getting shoved through a plate glass window and bleeding to death. The corresponding dream gave him the time, location and details on who had shoved the man. It would occur only a mile from the studio, so he walked the mile. It had begun as a minor argument that escalated. It was an easy save. Mark simply distracted the men from their argument by playing a lost tourist and butting into the argument to ask directions. They still appeared angry, so he inquired about a good restaurant, and before he left them, the men had forgotten the argument and were talking about where they would go for dinner.

It was a small victory. Mark shivered and shoved his hands in his jacket pockets, ducking his head against a blast of wind. He kicked a stone, enjoying the way it clattered and bounced on the pavement. When he caught up to it, he sent it ricocheting down the sidewalk again and smiled. He was in the mood to celebrate. Maybe he'd give Jessie a call and see if she wanted to go out.

Leaves whirled and spun down the sidewalk as he drew a deep breath of the frosty air feeling cleansed of his fear. He had to accept that September 11th had been too big for him to prevent. Twelve hours hadn't been enough time and he hadn't been prepared for something of that magnitude. He prayed to God that nothing like September 11th ever happened again, but if something did, he hoped that he could redeem himself by preventing it.

* * * * *

The End

Mark's story continues in:
NO GOOD DEED:
Book One in the Mark Taylor Series.

Read the first chapter of No Good Deed beginning on the next page.

Mark Taylor discovers first hand that no good deed goes unpunished when the old camera he found during a freelance job in an Afghanistan bazaar gives him more than great photos. It triggers dreams of disasters. Tragedies that happen exactly as he envisions them. He learns that not only can he see the future, he can change it. Then the unthinkable happened and everyone ignored his frantic warnings. Thousands die. Suddenly, the Feds are pounding on his door and the name they have for Taylor isn't urban hero. It's enemy combatant.

He finds himself locked in the brig with no rights, no trial, and no way out. Mark learns that being labeled an enemy combatant means they can do anything they want to him. Anything at all.

.

NO GOOD DEED
BOOK ONE IN THE MARK TAYLOR SERIES

BY M.P. MCDONALD

Cover Art by Imogen Rose

Special thanks to Dianna Morris and Jessica Tate for their help and encouragement.

Dedicated to my husband, Robert and my three children, Brian, Tim and Maggie.

CHAPTER ONE

The baby floated face down in the tub. The image hadn't changed, not that Mark Taylor expected it to. Not yet anyway. He tucked the photo in his back pocket and trotted down the steps from the 'L' platform. With any luck at all, the next time he looked, the baby would be fine. He skirted around an old lady tottering in his path and glanced at his watch.

All he had to do was find the apartment, convince the mom that he wasn't a nut case, or worse—a peeping tom—just because he knew that her phone would ring and distract her from bathing her daughter. Yep. Nothing complicated. Just get in, alert the mom, and get out. Five minutes, tops. Mark jogged, cursing under his breath at the rush of people heading towards the train station. The crowd thinned, and he broke into a sprint, his breath exploding out in a cloud of white.

Cars blocked the crosswalk, trapped there when the light turned red. *Shit.* He paced left, then right, willing the light to change. To hell with it. He darted into the street, ignoring the blasting horns. It wasn't like the cars could advance anyway. He stumbled when one bumped his thigh, or he bumped it. He wasn't sure which and didn't have time to find out. Limping, he raced on.

Mid-block, he slowed to read the address numbers set above the entrance of an apartment building. This was the one. He pivoted and took the short flight of concrete steps two at a time and tugged at the door. Locked. Of course.

Bracing his hands on the door, he panted. *Think*. There had to be a way in. He wouldn't fail. Not this time.

He swiped his hand down a panel of numbered call buttons, not caring who answered as long as someone let him in. "Come on...come on."

"Who is it?"

"Hey buddy, I forgot my key." It was the first thing that came to him and it didn't work. The next lie didn't either. Unable to think up a plausible story, he resorted to the truth on the fourth response. "It's an emergency! Life or death."

Maybe his voice sounded as desperate as he felt, or maybe the person didn't give a damn—whatever the reason, the guy let him in. He blinked as his eyes adjusted to the dimness. It was the second floor. He was sure of that. The dream played in his head like a movie, showing him the silver number twenty-two nailed to the door.

There was an elevator, but it was on the fifth floor. He spotted the stairs and flew up them, grabbing the railing to make the tight turn up to the second flight. It occurred to him that the door to the hallway might be locked, but luck was on his side this time and it opened. Bent in a runner's stance, hands on knees, he huffed and glanced at the number on the door nearest him. Twenty-three. He guessed left and turned in that direction. He raised his hand to knock, but froze when an anguished scream raised the hairs on the back of his neck.

"Christy!"

Startled, he stumbled back, bumping against the wall opposite the door. He was too late. He spun and slammed the side of his fist against the wall, a curse ready to explode off his tongue, when he heard fumbling at the door behind him.

"Help me! Someone!"

At the desperate plea, he lunged to the closed door. "Hello? You okay?" He knew it was a stupid question. Of course things weren't okay.

The door cracked open before a young women clutching a limp, gray baby, elbowed it wide. "My baby." Wild, desperate eyes met Mark's. "Please..."

Mark swallowed the acid in his throat and instinctively reached for the infant. "What happened?" He couldn't let on that he already knew. That led to questions he couldn't answer.

"I forgot her in the tub!" She clutched the baby and gave her a shake. "Oh god! Christy! She's not breathing!"

"I know CPR—give her to me." His sharp tone sliced through the mother's shock and she released her daughter with a wail of grief.

Mark positioned the baby with her head in his hand, her bottom in the crook of his arm.

The mother keened with her hands balled in front of her mouth. "Help her!"

The poor woman was teetering on the edge of hysteria, not that Mark could blame her. He was toeing the line himself, but he couldn't cross it. Not if there was a chance of saving the baby. With his free hand, he caught the mother's arm and gave it a firm squeeze. "I'm gonna help her, but you gotta listen to me. You need to call 9-1-1. Got it?"

She tore her gaze from her daughter, nodded, and raced back into her apartment. Mark wracked his brain, searching for a scrap of CPR knowledge that he knew was there. He cringed at the baby's glassy stare and blue-tinged lips. Her legs dangled lifelessly over his arm.

ABCs. That was it! Airway, breathing and circulation. He didn't see any water in her mouth, so her airway seemed okay. He covered her miniature nose and mouth with his own, feeling like a big clumsy oaf. Her scent filled his nose—so clean and innocent, like baby shampoo and powder. A damp, silky tuft of her hair tickled his cheek. If she died, it'd be his fault. He could have prevented this. He blew again. There wasn't time to worry about guilt now.

Her chest rose with the breaths and he felt it move against his arm. Out of the corner of his eye, he saw doors down the hall opening, and a small crowd gathered around him. Some shouted instructions, and a deep voice ordered someone to the lobby to let the paramedics in when they arrived.

There was no change in Christy's color. Shit. Those paramedics better get here pronto. Why didn't someone else step forward to do the CPR? Hell, there had to be someone more qualified. There was supposed to be a pulse point near the elbow, but hell if he could find it. It wasn't like he'd ever searched for one on a healthy kid before, let alone one who might not have one. Was that it? He prodded the inside of her arm, but between his shaking hands and the pudgy cushion at the bend of her elbow, he couldn't feel a beat.

Go to the source. He put his ear to her chest. Nothing. He swallowed hard as he placed two fingers on her breastbone and pushed down. The feel of her tiny chest caving in with each compression made his stomach churn.

He lost count of the cycles of breaths and compressions. It seemed like forever before someone suggested he stop and check for a pulse again. The mom had returned to his side at some point. His vision had narrowed to Christy's little body cradled in his arms. Mom stroked Christy's forehead and pleaded with her to breathe.

Listen to your mama, sweetie. Breathe, dammit. Wait...was she pinker? Or was it wishful thinking? He paused the compressions, but gave another breath.

As he lifted her to listen for a heartbeat, Christy blinked.

Startled, he jerked his head back and glanced at the mom to see if she'd noticed it too. Her eyes, full of anguish and fear, lit with a spark of hope as she met his look. It hadn't been his imagination.

Christy shuddered, and then coughed. Mark sat her up as she gagged, worried she was choking. She rewarded his efforts by puking sour milk down the front of him. She cried then, the sound as soft as a newborn kitten's. Impulsively, he kissed the top of her head.

A cheer rose in the hallway, and Mark glanced around, astonished to see so many people. A grin tugged at the corners of his mouth. The mother took her daughter from Mark, but planted a kiss on his cheek. The elevator at the far end of the hall opened, and paramedics stepped out.

Sure. Now *they show up.* Mark laughed, unable to suppress the giddiness. He took a deep breath, and leaned against the wall, his knees wobbling like Jell-O. He swiped his arm across his forehead. It was like a damn sauna in here. People crowded around, slapping Mark's shoulders and pumping his hand. Someone handed him a towel and he used it to mop up the mess on the front of his leather jacket, but there wasn't much he could do for the bit that leaked inside.

"Good job, man!" The speaker looked to be early to mid-thirties, close to Mark's own age. "That was awesome!"

"Thanks." Mark opened his mouth to ask if he could use a bathroom to wash up, when his stomach lurched and the bitter taste of bile filled his mouth. Panic surged through him and he rushed into the nearest apartment with an open door. He spotted a hallway and found the bathroom just in time for his lunch to make a return visit.

Spitting out the vile taste, he flushed the toilet and moved to the sink to wash, scooping some water into his mouth and swishing it around. He dried his hands on a towel hanging over the shower curtain. He reached for the doorknob, but stopped and pulled the photo out of his back pocket, just to make sure. The picture had only one similarity with the one he'd put in his pocket only minutes before. The baby was still Christy, but now, she was grinning at the camera, showing off two pearly white bottom teeth. It was official. He'd erased another photo.

There was a knock on the door a second before Mark opened it.

"You okay?" It was the guy from the hall. He leaned against the doorway, arms crossed.

Mark nodded and motioned towards the toilet "Yeah. Just feeling the nerves. Sorry for barging in."

The man laughed and stuck out a hand. "No problem. I'm Jason."

"Mark." He clasped the man's hand and gave it a shake.

Jason gave Mark a speculative look. "A few minutes before that happened," he pointed his chin towards the hall, "someone buzzed my apartment, saying they had to get in—that it was an emergency."

Mark tried to play it cool as he edged towards the hallway. "Yeah?"

"That was you, wasn't it?" It was a statement, not a question.

"I...uh..."

Jason waved a hand and cut him off. "No worries, dude. I was just curious. I had a grandfather who used to get premonitions. It was spooky. Never thought I'd meet someone else like that. Glad I let you in."

Rattled and still shaking from the flood of adrenaline, Mark could only nod. He breathed a sigh of relief when Jason motioned for him to go first as they went out to the hall.

They watched as the paramedics started an IV on the protesting Christy, and he winced at the blood oozing around the IV site. Poor little thing. He felt a tap on his shoulder and turned to find a Chicago police officer behind him.

"Sir, can I ask you a few questions?"

Mark shoved his hands into his pockets to hide the shaking and shrugged. "Sure."

He asked Mark's name and for some ID. After speaking some cop code into his shoulder radio, he glanced at Mark's driver's license. "You don't live here, so why were you in the building?"

Mark pulled at the collar of his shirt under his coat. Necessity forced him to lie in these situations and he hated it, but the truth was far too complicated. Experience allowed his story to slip easily off his tongue. "I intended to visit a friend, and when I got to the building, someone was coming out, so rather than buzz, I just caught the door. When I got up here, I realized I had the wrong building." He forced a laugh. "My buddy's building looks

a lot like this one and I guess I got them mixed up." Mark shook his head and rubbed the back of his neck. He was rambling and decided to cut the explanation short. "It's about time my faulty memory came in handy."

Luck was with him and the officer chuckled. "It sure did. You did a great job."

Mark dipped his head as heat rushed up his cheeks. "Thanks."

The cop's radio squawked, and in the midst of indecipherable code, Mark heard his own name.

The officer cocked his head, his gaze fixed on Mark as he reached up to key the mic. "10-9?"

The message was repeated and the officer tensed, his eyes cold as he acknowledged it and requested back-up. With one hand hovering over his weapon, he pointed at Mark with the other. "Turn around and place your hands on the wall."

Confused, Mark hesitated. "What...why?"

"Hands on the wall. Now!"

The commanding tone jolted Mark into action and he nearly tripped in his haste to comply. "Listen, sir, can I just ask—"

"We can do this the easy way or the hard way. The officer grabbed Mark's arm. "I've been told to bring you in for questioning."

"Who wants to talk to me? Why?"

The few people still milling in the hallway fell silent.

The cop glanced at the watching crowd and hesitated. "Unpaid parking tickets."

Parking tickets? Since when did they go to this much trouble for parking tickets? What the hell was going on? He twisted to see the cop's face. "I don't owe on any tickets. What's this really about?"

Jason stepped forward and pulled out his wallet. "Look, officer, the dude just saved a baby. What does he owe? I'll pay it."

"Step aside; this isn't any of your affair."

"Come on, man, don't be a hard-ass." Jason smiled at the cop, and gestured towards Mark. "I mean, this guy doesn't exactly look like Charles Manson."

Jason's attempt at humor backfired when the cop offered to let Jason accompany Mark.

Jason glared at the cop before casting an apologetic look at Mark. "Sorry. I tried."

Mark nodded. His face burned as the bystanders—the same people who'd cheered him just a few minutes before—now pointed fingers, and whispered to each other.

The cop's fingers dug into Mark's bicep. "Come on. You got some people waiting to meet you."

"Who?" This was going way too far for a few tickets that he couldn't even remember getting. "You sure you got the right Mark Taylor?"

The fingers tightened again as the cop frog-marched him towards the elevator. Mark balked. This was crazy. When the cop pressed him forward, he didn't think, he just reacted, jerking his arm free. "Quit pushing me!" The second the words left his mouth, he wanted to suck them back in.

"Get down! Right now. On your knees." The cop pulled his baton and prodded Mark with it.

"Whoa! Calm down. I just want to know the truth. I have that right, don't I?"

"I'm not going to tell you again." The radio blasted a sharp tone, and Mark started at the sudden noise.

The cop mistook Mark's reflex and swung the baton. Mark ducked his head and the blow landed with a thud against his shoulder. Pain rocketed down his arm like he'd touched a live wire. He sank to his knees. Two more blows landed on his back. He bit his lip to keep from crying out as he fell face-down on the floor, his nose buried in the dank, musty carpet.

The bystanders yelled at the cop while the cop shouted for them to shut up. Without pausing, the officer ordered Mark to lie down. Confused, Mark attempted to lift his face away from the nasty floor to tell him he was already lying down, but a sudden sharp pressure in the middle of his back pinned him to the floor.

He fought to breathe as his arms were wrenched behind him and cuffed. He managed to turn his head, the skin on his face pulling painfully taut as he sucked in air.

The door from the stairwell burst open and three more officers ran towards them, pulling their batons as they charged down the hall. Two men in suits followed, their manner and attitude exuding an aura of power and authority.

The first to reach Mark flashed a badge at him, but Mark couldn't get a clear look from his angle on the floor.

"I'm Special Agent Johnson and this is Special Agent Monroe. We have a warrant for your arrest as a material witness to terrorist acts against the United States."

ACKNOWLEDGMENTS

I wouldn't have been able to finish this book without the help of so many people. First and foremost, I would like to thank Jessica Tate. For about four years now, we've been pushing each other to write via our online writing sessions. I'm not sure what I would do without that push.

Thank you to my fantastic editor, Felicia Sullivan. Wonderful job!

Without my amazing beta readers, this book would have been a complete mess. What I found interesting was that all of them had different strengths. One was great at noticing missing words--and you'd
be surprised how often that happens as my mind thinks faster than my hands can type—another caught various plot point issues. Several zeroed in on my many typos, and one was a comma guru. So, in no special order, I'd like to thank, Vicki Boehnlein, Al Kunz,, and Allie Brumley.

And last, but not least, a huge thank you to my 'forumily'. You all know who you are. I love that there is a place I can go to get support, feedback, vent, or just get a much needed laugh. You are all awesome!

About the Author

I know a lot of these are written in third person, but that just feels too unnatural for me so I'm going to be a rebel and write this in first person. I'm M.P. McDonald, and I live in a small town in Wisconsin with my family, just a stone's throw from a beautiful lake, and literally spitting distance to a river on the other side. We love the peace and quiet and being able to go down to the beach on a hot summer day for a quick swim. Chicago and Milwaukee are just an hour's drive away in either direction, so we are never far from the excitement of a big city.

As you can tell from my books' setting, I love Chicago. One of my sons used to do commercials and modeling in the 90s, so we spent many an afternoon driving to auditions and look-sees there. Mark Taylor's studio/loft is based in part, on the many cool photography studios we encountered during his years in 'showbiz'.

When I'm not writing, I work as a respiratory therapist at a small hospital that is part of a large hospital system in eastern Wisconsin. I am currently full-time, which makes it kind of hard to find as much time to write as I would like, but I recently requested a switch to part-time and that will go into effect very shortly. For me, that is the best of both worlds! I enjoy my job as a therapist, and yet I want more time to write, so I am lucky that I will be able to do both.

I love to hear from readers. No, I mean it. I *love* to hear from readers, even if it's not all good. Without feedback from readers, I might never have undertaken this book. I hadn't planned on writing a series for Mark Taylor, but readers kept asking, so I was happy to deliver. I have an unrelated book I've put on the back-burner twice now in order to complete the last two books in this series. I'm hoping to finish that one soon and possibly start a fourth book in the Mark Taylor series.

CONTACT ME

Here are some ways you can reach me, and since I am an internet junkie, I'll probably write back very quickly.

Email: mmcdonald64@gmail.com
Facebook: http://www.facebook.com/pages/MP-McDonald/143902672336564 I am especially active on my FB page, with updates on book progress, and an occasional book contest, but mostly, it's awesome because of the amazing readers who are incredibly supportive We have a good time there, so come and join us!
Twitter: @MarkTaylorBooks
Pinterest: http://pinterist.com/mpmcdonald

Find the other books in the series currently available on Amazon:

No Good Deed: Book One in the Mark Taylor Series
March Into Hell: Book Two in the Mark Taylor Series
Deeds of Mercy: Book Three in the Mark Taylor Series

Made in the USA
San Bernardino, CA
29 January 2019